DEVIANT DEATH

Ruth Stanton is a famous crime novelist who has just returned from another foreign research trip. Her husband has stayed at home as usual and whilst she has been away, two women from the village have disappeared. One is Olive, the landlord Bill Lynch's wife and one is Judy, his lover.

If they are dead, where have the bodies been hidden? There would be plenty of hiding places around in the countryside. If the murderer or murderers are within the small Derbyshire community – a very close one – which of the locals are closing ranks?

DEVIANT DEATH

Gwen Moffat

First published 1973
by
Victor Gollancz Ltd

This edition 2000 by Chivers Press
published by arrangement with
the author

ISBN 0 7540 8577 5

British Library Cataloguing in Publication Data available

Printed and bound in Great Britain by
Redwood Books, Trowbridge, Wiltshire

PART I

Chapter 1

THE TOAST MASTER prayed for silence and Mrs Stanton rose to her feet gracefully, conscious of the correctness of things: the new suit, her hair, the expectant hush. Beyond a sea of brilliant hats the waiters stood at ease, for the most part attractive and all deferential, while out of the corner of her eye she saw that her own figure was centred accurately on a television screen —in colour.

She started with confidence. She was an excellent speaker, touching on the bizarre in her trade, but not the grisly, chilling their blood but never deep-freezing them. The feathers and flower petals shivered with laughter, and from behind her came the discreet chuckle of the toast master. Her back in its fine orange wool moved appreciatively, cat-like.

Ruth Stanton was a crime novelist and, in a sense, her income depended on murder, or at least on killing. She gave a little dissertation here, based on the premise that 'murder' was premeditated; killing often earned the verdict of manslaughter. Thus she passed to the thrills of *crimes passionnels*—but with the corollary that these had declined sadly since the early nineteenth century. What was Crippen even but a foolish and hen-pecked little man and what was Belle but a doomed victim? It was rather surprising that she could pass from

7

such amusing accounts of violent death to suggesting quite seriously that there had been a shift in moral values, but then she was a past mistress of design in public speaking.

An editor, svelte in aubergine velvet, whose lip had curled slightly as she noted that Ruth's crimes of passion stopped short of the men (and women) who were really outrageous, who had gone off into a daydream in which she was calculating the cost of that orange suit, was suddenly caught napping as her neighbour said loudly: 'Hear, hear!'

'...no question,' Ruth was saying, 'but that the ultimate blasphemy deserves the ultimate deterrent.'

'Good God!' the editor exclaimed. She was a liberal in private.

'Just what we needed,' grated her neighbour, a wiry policewoman, glaring at the editor's dark glasses. 'It's high time someone in the public eye had the courage to put their cards on the table.'

And then with a neat twist Ruth was back from the edge of the pit, praising the forces of law and order, the high-ranking policewomen of whom so many were present, the social workers ... was she going to include everyone? The Press came in for an accolade, but all with an emphasis on femininity, and the aubergine editor blushed with her neighbour, for the husky voice seemed truly grateful to these guardians of society. People smiled with misty eyes and for a moment the only movement in the huge room, faithfully reflected in the television screens, was the speaker seating herself, then the applause broke and agile young men in pastel suits were running and crouching in front of the table, aiming cameras, and people called imperatively: 'This way, Miss Stanton!' and 'Head up a shade, *please*, dear.'

A man's hand appeared at her elbow holding an envelope bearing her name. Leaning sideways, politely smiling for her neighbour's congratulations, and for the Press, she opened the note.

'I adore you,' it said without preamble. 'It has been a long cold summer and if you don't come at three o'clock I shall throw myself in the Thames leaving a note for the Coroner, telling all. I am in the foyer.'

It was unsigned.

She glanced at the television screens but the cameras were on the body of the room. She wondered when they had left her.

The marchioness rose and thanked her guests, paying extra tribute to the star speaker. Ruth inclined her head in acknowledgement. The ladies started to disperse, the top table letting the masses away before them.

'I have read all your books,' the wiry policewoman assured her as they edged towards the door.

'Not *all* of them!' Ruth laughed in delight.

'Ah, but you see: after I had read the thrillers, I had to read your travel books. Do you still travel?'

'I got back from Yugoslavia this morning.'

'Really. And you came straight here.'

'Almost. Just time to buy clothes.'

'What energy you must have. You farm in Derbyshire, don't you?'

'No. I live in a farmhouse but we don't farm—just write.'

'I don't think I remember.... You must eclipse your husband completely. What does he write about?'

'The Jebbs,' Ruth said absently, pushing into a gap, then they were blocked again. 'They were the oldest family in the dale and, in fact, it's their house we live in. It's a historical novel,' she elaborated to the officer, who clung to her like an indomitable terrier. Ruth wondered if the woman would make a good detective. She

9

considered not, since she must be pushing fifty and still in uniform, but did the C.I.D. have ladies? She made a mental note to check.

They reached the doorway and traffic started to flow. She flashed a smile at the navy uniform, slipped round the crowd and up the stairs. A rangy woman in a pink trouser suit and clubbed grey hair raced after her.

'Been trying to get a word with you—'

Ruth didn't pause and her smile was a trifle stiff.

'How long have you been back in England?'

'Seven hours.'

'What were you doing in Yugoslavia?'

'Research for my next book.'

'Is it true that you've sold the film rights of *Question in the House* for twenty-five thousand?'

'That was months ago.'

'I'm just checking.'

'It was five figures, I believe. I leave my business to my accountant.'

'What are you going to do now?'

They came to the main stairs above the foyer. Ruth slowed down and descended casually. She saw the man as soon as he stood up and before he came forward. Her eyes softened.

'Thank you,' she said kindly to the rangy woman, and turned away to hold out her hand to her lover.

'I'm so glad you could meet me, Mrs Stanton,' Paul Trevena gushed effusively, holding her hand and peering at her from behind pebble spectacles. 'Would you care for a pot of tea?'

The reporter retreated, staring suspiciously.

'My God,' Ruth said, leading the way to a corner and collapsing on a sofa. 'How lovely to be home. Public life gets you in the end. I'm devastated.'

He smiled at her with warmth and his voice was natural now that they were alone.

'It was worse for me; I was on the receiving end, praying that nothing would go wrong.'

'What?'

'Closed circuit telly. They had a room fixed up for the speeches. What on earth were you up to?'

'I shall probably never get the chance again to address the Women of the Year.'

'Just as well; this feminine backlash stuff won't do, you know. You'll lose all the kids and the intellectuals if you go on like this.'

She smiled lazily.

'Do I have to care?' Seeing his expression she went on quickly: 'No, I'm not being reckless, darling; I only touched on the serious aspects—'

A middle-aged waiter materialised with tea and the Savoy's exquisite sandwiches.

'If you'll allow me to say so, madam, an excellent speech.'

He said it out of the corner of his mouth, but with feeling.

'How kind of you,' she murmured. 'I do like appreciation.'

Paul dispensed tea neatly.

'Obviously,' he grumbled with a touch of jealousy, 'I was mistaken. You'll never lose anyone. You knock 'em down with one hand, pick 'em up with the other.'

'Not the same people.'

'You could. And how do you set about convincing *me* that capital punishment is right?'

She looked at her hands and her one ring: a cluster of rough gold set with navy sapphires.

'I'm so tired of murder,' she admitted at last, and she sounded exhausted. 'Tired of theory. One suddenly

11

wakes up to the fact that one's living in a fantasy world where violence takes place only inside books—and in one's mind. But it happens in reality. Look at the gangs. If there hasn't been a gang murder in London while I've been abroad, it's because it wasn't necessary to knock someone off. What about kidnappings? People used to try to preserve their victims to get the ransom money but now they're often killed. Sometimes I wonder if the idea behind kidnapping, and hi-jacking too, is not money or someone's freedom, but the ghastly excitement of the act itself, which centres round violence and death.' She shivered. 'It's anarchy, darling; it has to be stopped.'

'If one admits you're right,' he said grudgingly, 'there must be degrees of culpability. In your speech you mentioned the difference between murder and killing.'

'That was merely as an introduction to sex crimes. Not the nasty ones,' she corrected herself hurriedly, 'but the more tasteful acts.'

'I beg your pardon?'

'You know what I mean. There are some crimes I'd refuse to discuss even with you but ladies who shoot their erring husbands or lovers are quite permissible.'

'But you'd hang them all?'

'Well ... every case must be judged on its merits ...'

'Some day,' he said, helping himself to sandwiches, 'you're going to get involved in murder and the mind boggles at your reactions. Some day perhaps you'll murder.' He looked at her hopefully but shook his head. 'No, you have no feelings, and you're rich. You have nothing to kill for. But I'd like to be there when your theories are put to the test.'

She sparkled mischievously. Her moods were changing constantly for she was still suffering from euphoria following a minor triumph.

'Can you imagine it?' A shadow crossed her face. 'It

might be better not to. What do you suggest we do now? We haven't time for a gallery.'

'Go and see the ducks.'

She regarded him with appreciation.

'You always do the right thing.'

'Naturally,' he said primly. 'I love you.'

It was Indian summer in St James's Park, with a soft blue sky above the domes of Whitehall and the trees starting to change colour after an early frost. But it was still warm in the sun as they strolled beside the water arguing on an old theme.

'I don't want to spoil your home-coming,' he was saying, 'but what kind of a home-coming is it?'

She raised her eyebrows. She enumerated, half in play:

'An intelligent and healthy daughter, a pleasant home in a dale not yet discovered by the hordes—' She faltered but, collecting herself, grinned engagingly: 'There are friends and a career. . . .'

'Go on,' he urged.

'A husband.'

He said nothing.

'Who doesn't make pots of money—' she was on the defensive: '—but who's happy to stay in the country, and look after the house, and be a good father. We also get on,' she added with asperity. 'Which is more than you and I are doing. What's biting you?'

'Ned is a drone,' he said heavily.

'What on earth do you mean by that?'

'How much does he earn?'

'When did you start thinking success was measured in money terms?'

'Look ducky, it's got to be measured somehow, hasn't it? Standard of output can be another criterion, but most people would postulate some output in the first place.'

'Oh, there's output. He's done over two hundred thousand words, or had before I left.'

'*What!*'

'Well, it's practically the history of a dale, and the Jebbs were pretty prolific; he's still researching the third volume.'

'The what?'

'It's a trilogy now. I suggested it. It has the advantage that he can get two volumes into print without waiting for the whole thing to be finished.'

'Oh. And who is his publisher?'

'He's shopping around.'

'Meaning everyone he's approached so far has turned it down. You're not kidding yourself—or me. And for my money, you're not kidding Ned either. There's only one person bringing in the lolly in that house. How do you think he feels to see you driving a Jensen while he puts up with a Mini? Come to think of it, who paid for the Mini?'

'I'd have to pay someone to look after the house if I hadn't Ned,' Ruth pointed out.

'And if you had a housekeeper you'd provide her with a car.' His tone changed. 'Ever wonder why Ned is obsessed with the environment?'

'I hadn't thought about it. Why?'

'You hadn't thought about it. Now, that's typical of you. I'll tell you why Ned's trying to find salvation through the anti-Concorde Project and heated digestion sewage plants: for the same reason that wives with successful men for husbands take up *macramé* and oil painting. Ned's bored, ducky, and he's a failure and you're rubbing his nose in it. Two hundred thousand words! My God.'

14

'You're bitchy today,' she remarked companionably. She stepped aside to avoid a barnacle goose and quickened her pace. He caught her up and took her arm.

'Look,' he said urgently. 'I sat in that place listening to you and watching you on the screen. You're dishy to look at despite your years and although you talk drivel sometimes, it always sounds delightful because you've got that voice, but you didn't talk drivel today; you were funny and a bit sick and you ended with everyone—well, nearly everyone—grateful to you. You've got star quality and you beat 'em to their knees and I watched them and wanted to shout out loud that you were my mistress —and I had to sit in the corner and keep quiet. I knew how the other woman feels at the posh family funeral of her lover. Catholic for choice.'

She stopped and kissed him.

'You're so corny sometimes I wonder if you're real,' she said.

'I want to marry you.'

'I'm not going to marry you.'

'You can do it under the new law: breakdown of marriage: irretrievable.'

'My marriage hasn't broken down, and I'm happy as I am.'

'I'm not, and you're being exploited.'

'By Ned? Don't be ridiculous.'

They passed a bevy of small children herded by dainty Nordic *au pairs* who looked little older than their charges. Paul surveyed them professionally.

'What about your girls?' Ruth asked.

'I have only one.'

'Marlene Beck?'

'Who's she?'

'Your assistant or something on the film you made in Panama.'

15

'I don't have *affaires* since I met you,' he corrected himself.

'Fortunately I'm not possessive.'

'With anyone else that would be leading up to a hell of a row about Marlene Beck. But you don't give a damn, do you?'

She stared across the water at the shadows darkening in the undergrowth on the other side. Two pelicans floated past.

'No,' she said, 'not about her. I might if you fell in love. Try me some time.' Her tone became businesslike and she urged him along the path. 'It's getting nippy and I need a drink and we've a tremendous amount to discuss. I'm going to the flat to change and then we'll feed at a place where we don't know anyone and I can tell you all about my new story.'

Ruth wasn't worried. Periodically they had the same argument. He was a great film director but he was neither sophisticated nor clever. Like her, he worked from instinct and, when at times he had to concentrate on technique, he was competent but no longer great. He liked to be sure of what he was doing and then he followed through with confidence. It was the same in his private life. So, in love with Ruth, he wanted her to stay with him. Marriage was a way of keeping her.

This was how she saw it but she was quite happy with the position as it was, and so long as Paul didn't get uppity, the situation could remain pleasant, with only a periodic argument which, even if he had been a little more vehement today (an *affaire* that went wrong while she was abroad perhaps?) could still be handled.

She observed him as he studied the menu in the small and very expensive restaurant they'd discovered last spring: the thick black hair greying prematurely,

16

the pugnacious frog's jaw that twitched in anticipation as he concentrated on food. Concentration, she thought; it's his forte. Mine too. We know what we want and we go all out for it—and get it. Poor Ned, he's a dabbler.

He looked up quickly and caught her eye:

'What is it?'

'I was thinking about people who are the last of long lines,' she lied. 'Like Emily Jebb.'

'So?'

'Things get concentrated: characteristics. The Jebbs were always highly individualistic—and look at Emily. They were loyal, stubborn and partisan. So's Emily. They were good farmers and stockmen. Emily can do wonders with a sour patch of land or a sick horse.'

'But the end of a line can become diffused too.'

They both knew he was thinking of her husband, who had been a Jebb on his mother's side.

'How much did you spend on your house, Ruth?'

'You mean what did I pay Emily for it, or what have we spent on it since?'

'It was an idle question, and impertinent. Forget it.'

'I wouldn't mind answering but I haven't the remotest idea. It didn't cost much twelve years ago. It seemed a lot then, of course; I can't remember whether it was three or four thousand. But as to what I—we've spent on it since! It's a nice investment, though,' she ended cheerfully in extenuation for her extravagance.

'I can't think how Emily could have come to sell Heathens' Low.'

When Uncle Mason Jebb died and left Catcliff to her it was habitable, whereas Heathens' was terribly primitive. They carried water in droughts. It needed an enormous amount spent on it, but the money she got for it must have been very welcome. As for giving up Heathens' for Catcliff, it's all one to Emily whether she

17

lives in a Victorian pile or a nice farmhouse. She hasn't got much aesthetic taste, if any.'

'Like Laura. You've got some monstrosities in that dale.'

'Laura Eden!'

'Her house. I'm talking about houses. If I was talking about the owners, I'd say characters not monstrosities. Laura's house is a monument to money.'

'It's comfortable and warm, and now her trees are coming on, it's mainly hidden. And it's glorious when you're on the inside looking out, all that glass and light, and the fountain in summer. I think Yaffles is great fun.'

'Even the name sounds like a toy dog.'

'Yaffles are green woodpeckers and you know Laura isn't that kind of woman. It isn't sentiment makes her take in those horses. If you're campaigning against live shipment you've got to practise what you preach.'

'I would have thought it more practical if she built a slaughter-house at the point of embarkation but I see the reasoning—dimly. I agree, Laura's warm-hearted, but so far as taste goes, she's one with Emily. I wonder how John Eden takes to being housed by a rich wife.'

'At a guess, he never thought about financial portions in his life,' Ruth said. 'He's a competent doctor and since he works hard, presumably makes enough to support a family. Laura's money will be just a pleasant bonus to him. Laura and the boys will be what matters. Money's a side-issue.'

They both skirted delicately round Ned Stanton who, since he was pushed out of Fleet Street and married Ruth, could have made scarcely enough money from book reviews and the odd feature on country life to pay his petrol bill.

The wine list was presented and they deliberated

carefully on the merits of a white burgundy as opposed to hock.

'I like your neighbours on the whole,' Paul resumed when the waiter had gone.

'They weren't a matter of luck. We did choose the place partly because of the people. I know it's Ned's home valley, but we could have bought a place in another dale. But having spent our honeymoon at the Quiet Woman, and then going back for weekends, we knew everyone (I mean, I did; Ned had always known them, of course); knew them before Emily decided to move from Heathens' Low to Catcliff. Ned always wanted to buy a house in Bardale. But I agree: we do have nice neighbours. We were lucky with the Edens in that the boys are the same age group as Sue and they're not hooligans, thank God, although we don't go in for hooligans in Bardale—well, not up at our end.'

'Dear Ruth, so respectable. And yet you depict violence so faithfully in your books.'

'That's different, isn't it? I don't like watching you make a film; it's too realistic, particularly with the good actors. I abhor violence in reality. Perhaps that's why I write about crime: sublimation; I'm sure it's why I love Derbyshire. It's so gentle. If Bardale had been presented to me objectively, without its being Ned's birthplace, I would still have chosen to live there.'

'You don't really live there, do you?'

'That's the point. It's my bolt-hole. I adore London and the travel and the research. That most of all, perhaps: creating a story out of people and a setting. But there are two scenes: the first, when the facts present themselves, geography, the local character and so on, then the second scene when all the material has been collected and you withdraw, and the story happens. It happens in Bardale.'

She drank her sherry. Her eyes were shining. He stared at her, his elbows on the table, his chin in his hands.

'You're a witch,' he said. 'You juggle with people and change their lives.'

'No, you manipulate more than I do. My characters are fictitious, only based on reality. In my mind they start to evolve from nucleii. You deal with real people.'

'Only superficially. I start with a nucleus, but it's an idea. I make a story too. The actors interpret it. It's the story that matters with me as well. I don't manipulate *people*; I direct parts of a story.'

Their dinner was served: paté and trout and lobster. They drank wine and the candles highlighted her copper hair.

'One would never think you had a girl of fourteen,' he said.

'Och, away! Ah was raped by the maister at thir-r-teen!' she cried in loud Glaswegian. A large woman in purple and silver Lurex froze and soup dribbled from her spoon.

'My dear!' Paul commiserated lugubriously.

'Ah've put it ahint me,' she assured him. 'Ahint,' she repeated, puzzled, under her breath.

'I should hope so.'

They toasted each other expressionlessly.

'So you'll come home with me,' she said quietly, continuing another conversation.

'I suppose I'll have to. If you won't stay at the flat, and we've got to get this Balkan thing worked out, and then I've got this idea about the quarry—'

'It won't work,' she said flatly. 'It's been done, and besides, it's not your *métier*, telly documentaries. Imagine: doing it in three parts so that models can drift in at intervals and chant something inane about detergents or oven cleaners!'

'I want to do it. It's worthwhile and it's topical.'

'The dale's not going to like it.'

'They won't know till it's shown. They'll think it's a film about the quarry, which in fact, it will be. I know they won't approve the conservation slant. After all, the dale's economy depends on the quarry, but when you come to think of it, the people in the Street will look at it objectively. Joe Hibbert's a naturalist even though he works in the quarry. Henry Raven will chuckle at the shareholders' discomfiture, Padley never has a good word for anything, even his own cattle. There's young Michael Hibbert, of course. You said there were no hooligans in Bardale. You forgot Michael.'

'I didn't. There's a difference. Michael isn't destructive. He went stealing—once. He's settled down since he married.'

'I haven't been home with you for nearly a year. Are they still next door to Joe and Annie?'

'Oh yes. Marilyn and Michael are still in the Street. I don't think Annie would let Michael move away, not without a fight. She wants to keep an eye on the company he frequents to make sure he doesn't revert to the friends who went to jail with him. Annie is fanatically Puritan and that jail sentence nearly broke her. Her health isn't too good either. It's fortunate Michael found a decent girl. Marilyn's tough under the prettiness, but she's sexy too. Makes the atmosphere down there a bit less rarified for Michael, I imagine.'

'I don't think the Street will mind about my documentary,' Paul said, not much interested in other people's problems. 'After all, it's unlikely that the quarry will go out of business simply because a few pipits and larks lose their nests every time a shot is fired.'

'Which they don't, anyway. A lot you know about pipits and larks. No self-respecting bird would nest within half a mile of that face. Everything's an inch thick in dust so there can't be any food for them, the ground must be sterile from the shock of the blasting, and the stone crusher's operational continuously. The only thing that makes it tolerable for us is that we're out of sight and sound of it. If one lived at Bull Low—well, one wouldn't live at Bull Low.'

'I'd like to get a picture of the face when they fire a shot. What a way to kill someone, if a mistake was made in the timing. Could they prove it was deliberate?'

He stared at her speculatively. She made a gesture of warding off the evil eye.

'No,' she cried, oblivious of the other diners. 'I won't. I've got Yugoslavia to do and then I'm having a holiday, a long one. Moreover, I won't experiment on my own doorstep. If you failed, if I failed, I couldn't go on living there. It would be a constant reminder of failure. I won't touch a script about the area. It's ludicrous anyway,' she continued more quietly. 'There's no story in Bardale. You'd have the devil of a job creating one. The Street's very ordinary: dark, dominated by the crags, rather claustrophobic, the people are that way inclined too: Joe and Michael and Padley—or they're neurotic like Annie or ailing like Henry with his multiple sclerosis. I suppose you might make something of Henry Raven sitting at his window all day watching the odd resident and the occasional tractor go by—but hell! you can't make a story out of the odd happening. Who'd murder whom and why?'

'If you had a Marie Stopes in the village, she could make a start with Judy Scroop.'

Ruth laughed delightedly.

'Poor Judy,' she said without pity. 'She had another this year.'

'How many does that make?'

'I've no idea. Hades Flatt is *bulging*. This latest baby might be the sixth.'

'Different father?'

'Never one the same according to Brenda. She seems to take a ghoulish pride in her daughter's career. But she's a marvellous grandmother. Come to that, Judy's not a bad mother, either. They're very happy children, if a little unruly.'

'Mad. A crazy, happy nympho. A contradiction in terms.'

'No. She's not a nympho. There's nothing neurotic about Judy. She likes sex and men and babies. She's got the I.Q. of a seven-year-old and the morals of a cat and she's the happiest woman in Bardale. It's a joy to have her working in the house.'

'What does Sue think?' he asked with his odd flash of primness.

'She accepts her in the same way that she accepts Emily's tortoiseshell queen who produces regularly three times a year—only, thank God, Judy does it less often than a cat—and the result is awaited with the same kind of interest to guess who the father is this time.'

'And Ned?'

'Ned?' She frowned. 'I don't know. It hadn't registered. He's never around when she is, I suppose.'

'You know, ducky, you've got blind spots. I never noticed it before.'

'Why should I notice how Ned looks at the help? She's an amusing nonentity. Like all the other chaps, he'll have tried her once and then forgotten about her. After all, you don't play around with someone in the same village when it's just possible she could slap a paternity order on you.'

'Apparently a fair number of men have taken the risk.'

'That's the answer. So long as she's promiscuous, there's no risk. In any case, Judy hasn't the brain or the inclination to go to court. All her brood are supported by the long-suffering ratepayers—and she gets a lot of my clothes too. She looks terrific in them.'

'Brenda would.'

'Would what?'

'Try to get a paternity order against a putative father.'

'Is that the term? Yes, she might.' She sounded doubtful. 'But they wouldn't stand a chance. Blood tests prove only negative parentage. Brenda wouldn't know that. Anyway, what are you worrying about? Ha!' She leaned across the table. 'I must go to Hades Flatt and look for the Trevena jaw, but don't worry, everyone down there is as happy as sandboys—or a litter of puppies, is more like it.'

Chapter 2

THE FIRST DROPS of rain fell as Emily Jebb was coming home across the big field called the Outlands but the rain didn't bother her. She left the track and mounted a stone stile in the wall to emerge on scorched turf above Magg's Tor. She frowned at the grass, then brightened. 'We can do with it,' she muttered referring to the rain. It had been a long hard summer.

Below the limestone cliff lay the Street of Town Head. At its foot, on her left, was the Quiet Woman and its small triangle of lawn, and at the side of the inn was the Scroop cottage: Hades Flatt. She could hear the new baby crying. Unusual, she thought, then the cries stopped. She nodded approvingly, not because she thought crying babies should be picked up but because Brenda Scroop did. Emily liked things to fit. A crying baby at Hades Flatt didn't.

Upstream the river showed pale through dull and thinning foliage. Immediately below Magg's Tor it was hidden behind the back yards of the Street. A bus ground uphill and stopped at Mrs Padley's shop. Susan Stanton dismounted. Emily knew it was her because it was the bus she always caught if there was no hockey or Drama after school. She saw by the girl's attitude that she was looking up. Emily waved, and Susan waved back, then she went into Mrs Padley's.

The bus turned at the top bridge, below Bardale Bank. This was the other road out of the dale: narrow, steep and badly-surfaced. The bus returned past the elder Hibberts', where Annie's washing hung in the back yard—so she couldn't be feeling too bad today—past Michael and Marilyn's, and Mrs Padley's shop. Then came John Eden's surgery, on the ground floor of the cottage where Mrs Padley stored non-perishable goods in the bedrooms. Last came the Ravens' house, with the parlour window tight closed against the cold air. Henry would be in front of the television set now, and Lily would be making tea.

The Street was deserted at this time of an autumnal afternoon, except for Susan, coming out of the shop and reading what from its size would be *Riding*. Fine plumes of smoke rose from chimneys, blue and pale in the dank shadow of the cliffs.

A raw breeze crept across the Outlands and Emily pulled her knitted cap lower on her ears. The old woman fitted her environment. She wore baggy trousers tucked into American parachutists' boots, and an old camouflaged anorak. White wisps of hair escaped from under her cap. She cut her own hair and it looked like it. She was well over sixty and her face, brown and wrinkled from exposure to wind, was like one of those studies of alpine crones in coffee table books. The fine grey eyes were magnified behind spectacles rimmed with plain steel. Emily had no time for the superfluous.

Now she climbed back over the stile and strode across the Outlands like a mountaineer.

There was a hump in the middle of the field and, as she topped this rise, a barn came in view: an isolated stone structure with its own yard and a closed gate. A Land Rover stood on the track.

She opened the gate and walked through the yard

of caked earth to a wicket at the top of a green path which disappeared steeply through the woods in the direction of the Quiet Woman. A few yards down the path a man was watching something, his profile towards her. She waited without speaking. After some moments he turned and came up the path: a big, powerful man in middle-age, moving like an animal. His face was as tanned as hers, and the pale eyes were startling in the dark face.

'Seen a goldcrest,' he said.

'No! When did we last have a goldcrest, Joseph?'

Joe Hibbert thought for a moment.

'Ten years back, before the big snow.'

'You saw just one?'

'Could be more. It were feeding with a flock of tits.'

'We couldn't have missed it if it nested here. It must be on passage.'

'Ay, you wouldn't a' missed it.' He smiled. It was a compliment.

'Is this a day off?' she asked.

'Yes, we're slackening a bit with the new motorway near finished. I thought I'd better take a day. Annie never sees me, she says.'

They went through the yard, Hibbert carefully closing the gates behind him. They stood beside the Land Rover and he nodded at the barn.

'Seen owls lately?'

'No. They're gone for good.'

'They'd come back.'

'They might,' she conceded. 'But not to be disturbed. There's a lot to be said for the old days and courting in the parlour, Joseph.'

He stared gloomily at the closed doors of the barn.

'Sort as comes up here a'n't always got a parlour. Empty, that is.'

27

A flurry of rain was borne on the rising breeze.

'Give me a lift home,' she ordered. 'I've left my windows open. And you must get back and tell Annie it's starting to rain, or her washing will be soaked. She may be asleep.'

From the barn, which was called Jagger's, the track bore right across the Outlands, away from the cliffs, then dipped from the central rise, and as the Land Rover bucketed down the ruts, a tiny hanging valley came in view with a stream in the bottom that would join the river at the bridge above the Street. This was Foodale. On the north side of it, facing the Outlands and half-hidden in the woods, were the three houses belonging to the Edens, the Stantons and Emily herself.

The Eden house was ranch-style, the brightness of cedar, the white trim and vast expanses of glass showing up richly even in the dusk. Then came Heathens' Low, Emily's old home, now owned by Ruth, with its limestone walls and gritstone slates, merging like a rock with the trees.

At the top of the dale Emily's present home, Catcliff, was dark, square and uncompromising, set in sombre shrubs, with a monkey puzzle incongruous among yellowing birches.

Drives curved from each house to the narrow metalled road that climbed the hill from Bardale. Hibbert stopped the 'Rover below Catcliff and Emily alighted. As she turned up the drive he called:

'Mrs Stanton's back tonight.'

'Yes.' She turned slowly and their eyes met. 'Yes,' she repeated. 'We'll all be glad to see her.'

'Sensible lady, no nonsense about her.'

The engine was running but he was in no hurry to get away.

Emily nodded.

'She won't stand any nonsense,' she agreed.

'She's got the whip hand, as you might say.'

'I don't like discord,' Emily Jebb said, speaking slowly and carefully. 'We shall have a fair bit of entertaining this weekend. Susan tells me her mother's bringing Mr Trevena. I want you to go down to Brenda Scroop after your tea and tell her I need Judy here tomorrow to give me a hand, and that I said the girl's to have an early night because there'll be a lot to do tomorrow.'

He nodded and reached for the gear lever.

'I'll try, but you'll have a job with that Judy.'

'You speak to Brenda,' she told him firmly. 'She'll do as she's told.'

The cloud level dropped with darkness and it set in for a wet night.

'Typical Pennine October,' Ruth commented as the white snout of the Interceptor nosed across the plateau where pale walls shone like glass on the bends. They saw no other cars and for a mile they'd seen no houses. All lights bar their own were invisible in the mist.

'We could be on an empty planet,' Paul said, savouring the idea with relish.

'You might turn on the radio.'

'No. I adore this. It's full of menace. What do you imagine's going on out there in the fog?'

But she didn't share his mood.

'I hope everything's all right,' she murmured.

'What d'you mean—everything?'

'The first rain after a long dry spell. Ned said on the phone they'd had no heavy rain since August. Old houses seem to shrink like deck planks. We always find leaks after a drought.'

The ground fell away and for a moment the lights

29

hung in space before the bonnet dipped and they saw the road again.

'Bardale Bank,' she observed.

'You're going too fast.'

'I know the road.'

The car lurched drunkenly and righted itself.

'Not that bit, you didn't!'

'They still haven't surfaced it,' she said with amused resignation. 'We ring the Council about once a week, all of us in turn, and they say they've got to do the roads that carry most traffic first. We've got a quarry working three shifts a day to take roadstone to the motorways and we can't have our own road metalled.'

The car eased down the steep gradient, sinking in pot-holes masked by wet drifts of leaves. It could have been a farm track. They came out below the cloud and the trunks of trees gleamed solidly on their right. Ruth turned left at the bottom, over the ancient pack-horse bridge with its low parapets, and the powerful car climbed the Foodale hill to turn in at the second gate. At last they saw lights beyond the slanting rain.

Ruth's daughter was doing her homework in the brilliant kitchen. She leapt up as they came in the door.

'Mum! You're early! How lovely. Did you have a good time? Gosh, you're brown—in *autumn*! It's not fair. How are you Paul? Can I be Anna in your "Karenina"?'

'I'm not—'

'You said so on telly last week—'

'You misunderstood me, like a hundred other nubile dollies. I said—'

'Where's Ned?' Ruth asked, making room on the table for her packages.

'Working. Shall I tell him you're here?'

But at that moment Ned Stanton opened the door.

Like Paul, Ruth's husband wasn't tall, only about five feet eight, but where Paul was solid, Ned was wiry. He had pale blue eyes which appeared to reflect his thoughts rather than what he saw, so that even when they brightened with enthusiasm, the enthusiasm was personal, not objective. Ned could be passionate but his passion was reserved for ideas rather than for people or the senses.

He had a huge black beard, grizzled like his hair. The beard was bushy because he wasn't concerned with appearances, but he wore his hair short because Ruth wanted him to; she said it suited him and made him look like a sea captain.

He was wearing a navy fisherman's jersey, jeans and espadrilles and as he came in the door he looked as if he'd just woken up.

'Nice,' he said vaguely. 'Nice to have you back.'

Ruth kissed his cheek.

'Lovely to see you, darling,' she said. 'Have we interrupted you?'

'Not really.' More firmly: 'Of course not. High time for a rest anyway.' He grinned at Paul. 'The besetting sin of the age: not knowing how to relax; that so, Paul?'

Paul nodded morosely.

Susan was investigating the shopping brought from London and Ned, childishly inquisitive, moved close to participate. Ruth watched her husband and daughter benignly. She smiled, caught Paul's cynical eye and her expression changed.

'You're full of calculation,' Paul said audaciously.

'What's that?' Ned asked, examining a garlic bulb with deep suspicion.

No one answered him. The business of unpacking continued, with Susan exclaiming in delight over favourite foods and Ned, equally intent and even more serious, completely ignoring his wife, not with any rudeness but simply because at the moment he was more interested in her shopping.

'We'll leave you two to unpack the car,' she said. 'We need a drink. Cloud's down on the plateau. We had to *crawl*. And I nearly broke the springs on Bardale Bank.'

'It's taken the sump off the Mini,' Ned said absently. 'Again?'

'It was the silencer last time. It's all right; it's mended now.' He looked up with a trace of anxiety: 'You're not mad?'

'Of course not. Well, I'm mad at the Council. If they don't mend that road—! Did you ring them?'

'No, I left that till you came back.'

'I'll do it tomorrow. I'll send them the bill for the sump too. Come on Paul—whisky.'

'Tell us everything that's happened,' she demanded.

They were sitting in the kitchen drinking coffee after a supper of cold fowl and salad. A bottle of Cointreau sat comfortably on the scrubbed table and Ruth was savouring her liqueur with deep pleasure.

Her daughter drew in her breath but threw a glance at Ned.

'Oh, the usual things, you know,' he said vaguely.

Susan rushed to the breach.

'You know all the important things like where we came in the Show and the gymkhana,' she began. 'But Emily's last litter included a Russian Blue,' she giggled wildly. 'That is, Vinya had the litter, of course. And the fox took one of Emily's White Wyandottes. A new pony came a week ago. It's terrible, Mum, you should see it—all sores, and so lame in its near fore it could hardly walk, but John's doing wonders with it and Laura's feeding it brewer's yeast and molasses.'

'What for?' Paul asked as she drew breath.

'Vitamin B and iron,' she told him indulgently.

'But what about people?' Ruth asked.

'Oh.' She paused. Paul and her mother stared at her in gentle amusement. She was an attractive girl with long, dark red hair and big violet eyes now clouded with the effort of remembering the less important issues.

'Yes,' she said slowly. 'Only little things, nothing sensational. That's unusual in three months, isn't it? Judy Scroop's baby is quite old now. Was it born when you left?'

'Yes.'

'It's growing to look like Renishaw,' Susan told them.

'P.C. Renishaw, from Bull Low? Never!'

'It is. The spitting image.'

'Rubbish!' Ned said angrily.

'Surely other things have happened?' Ruth prompted quickly.

'Well, you know Marilyn's—' She glanced at her father.

'Yes, we know who's pregnant in Bardale,' Ruth said firmly. 'No one died?'

'No. Mrs Lynch departed for pastures new. I'd forgotten her.'

'Mrs Lynch from the Woman? Why?'

'Judy Scroop.'

'It's no good,' Paul said, sighing. 'You just can't get away from her.'

'Well, folks—' Ned rose with forced heartiness. 'I have to get back to the grindstone, you know. If I don't see you again—goodnight.'

He left them and they drew together.

'Was Judy working at the Woman?' Paul asked.

33

'She always did, on and off,' Susan told him. 'They shared the cleaning between them, Brenda and Judy. But Mrs Lynch always saw to it that she was there in the mornings, so Bill Lynch was never alone before the pub opened. I suppose she thought it was safe to leave him on his own during licensing hours because he had to be available to serve customers.'

'You mean, the idea was never to leave him alone with Judy?' Paul translated.

'This conversation is unseemly,' Ruth remarked.

'Don't be square, Mum. I know everything.'

'I doubt it.'

Susan was incensed and continued with a self-righteous air:

'If you'd come back from the bank at four o'clock in the afternoon and found your husband locked in the loo and Judy Scroop making the bed when you always made it yourself after breakfast, you'd think a bit, wouldn't you?'

'Good Lord!' Ruth's eyes widened. 'What happened when he came out of the loo?'

'No one knows, but Mrs Lynch has shaken the dust off her feet. I expect she'll come back. It's a free house.'

'You cynical piece, you,' Paul expostulated. 'How do you know what happened, anyway?'

'Mrs Lynch gave Lily Raven a lift back from Sheffield that day and Lily went in the Woman with her to get Henry's medicinal brandy. Mrs Lynch lets her have it cheaper than the supermarket.'

'I'm glad she doesn't get it off the National Health,' Paul said reprovingly. 'As a ratepayer I would object strongly to paying for Henry's brandy. So Lily told Henry, who told Padley, who told Mrs P?'

'Did that old—lady tell you?' Ruth asked.

'No.' Susan looked at her mother steadily. 'You know,

Mum, anything that happens is all round the village in a moment. It's a bit sinister really. I know the Lynch business is funny but *they* don't think so. It's strange when you come to think of it. They all know, every detail, but there's no reaction. They kind of stifle it like a —you know: like something deformed that turns up in a litter. You put it down and bury it quickly.'

'That's a terrible way to talk.' Ruth was shocked.

'No, I don't mean *Judy*! I mean what happened down there: in the Woman. It was over a month ago, during summer. It's gone. They've forgotten it, put it out of their minds. I should have put it out of mine too.'

'But, ducky, it was a good story. Gossip's great fun. We thrive on it.' Ruth watched Paul comforting her daughter. She was puzzled.

'What were you reassuring her about?' she asked when Susan had gone to bed. 'I didn't follow that.'

'I think she felt a bit guilty about relaying that kind of intimate gossip when the rest of the village didn't.'

'But this is family. They'll talk in their own homes.'

'I'm not family,' he reminded her. 'In this context "family" means "village". You don't let it go outside. Susan is dales folk. I'm not. You're not really. And Ned was furious. It's as she said: if you're one of them you stifle it. You accept the village tart or the village idiot but you don't discuss them and you never laugh at them. They're slightly reprehensible, to be swept under the carpet, with the rest of the dirt.'

Ruth shuddered.

'Poor Judy,' she said. 'I never felt sorry for her before.'

'Like I said: you just don't know how the other half lives, with your Habitat kitchen and your Paris clothes and your stone-ground bread. Gentle Bardale! Bardale's a hotbed of violent, seething passions about to erupt—'

he glanced towards the window and shrugged, '—when it stops raining.' He turned to her, the light striking his glasses. 'Where's Olive Lynch?'

'I don't know.' She was amused but tired. 'Have a Cointreau for the road.' She held up the bottle.

'I'll tell you where she is. In Bill Lynch's vegetable patch. You go and look at his potatoes tomorrow. Bet you a quid they're wilting.'

'If Bill Lynch has got any sense he'll have lifted his potatoes a month ago—and you don't bury your victims in Bardale. You put them down Styx Hole.'

He was arrested in mid-flight, astonished.

'Of course you do,' he breathed. 'How clever of you. I'll have that Cointreau now.'

Chapter 3

RUTH SLEPT IN a room of her own with the window open wide and she was wakened at dawn by muttered but desperate curses. She listened, then closed her eyes again. There was a crash of breaking glass.

'Oh, my God!' Someone was at the end of their tether.

She got up and went to the window. Laura Eden, solid and incongruous, wearing an old Burberry over peach brushed nylon, was examining the leg of a pony that could have modelled for Death's mount in Doré's *Apocalypse*. The hoof was planted firmly on the remains of a cloche.

Ruth retreated silently and dressed. Sounds of splintering shards came from below. She opened the back door and emerged to find the doctor's wife tugging vainly at a depleted forelock.

'You'll scalp it,' Ruth said. 'Here.' She held out a bridle.

'Put it on, love,' Laura gasped. 'He's a bit nervy. Didn't want to wake you. When did you get back? You're looking well. I owe you a cloche and some chives. He plonked a great foot on your herb border. Looks like a mule, doesn't he?' She pulled a long ear affectionately.

'Someone gave him a beating,' Ruth observed, studying long scabs on the animal's haunches.

'Odd, isn't it? Could you whip a horse hard enough

37

to bring the hair off? You know, if you're not accustomed to violence, you can't identify wounds, can you? The R.S.P.C.A. man would know— Sorry, love,' as she caught Ruth's eye. 'Just before breakfast too.'

'Come in and have coffee.'

'Black Roast? Did you bring some for me?'

'Pounds of it.'

'Angel! I'll put him in your loose box.'

'What's this about Olive Lynch?' Ruth asked as they drank her scalding black brew.

'My dear! You heard? Sue, of course. She'll know more than me. I never have Judy, you know that, because of the boys. She'd eat them. Marilyn comes when she's not here at Heathens' but she's too respectable, at least superficially, to gossip about Judy. Tell me what *you* know.'

Ruth did so, leaving out Paul's wild guess concerning the whereabouts of Mrs Lynch.

'Something will have to be done about Judy Scroop,' Laura said. Her plump face was serious under its film of nourishing cream.

'Perhaps John—?' Ruth suggested delicately.

'Well, *something*.'

'It's difficult.' Ruth sighed for Laura who had such a strong social conscience. 'But is it doing any harm? I mean, the kids are all bright enough, much brighter than Judy. If it weren't for the rather unconventional background, that household would be a model for a good many at Bull Low.'

'But *now*! When we're all campaigning for population stability! She's only twenty-five!'

'It's an isolated instance. And to tell you the truth,' Ruth added firmly, 'it's totally outside my control, so I wash my hands of it.'

'Well, you're all right. You haven't got any boys.'

Laura looked uncomfortable. 'And Ned's always absorbed in the Jebbs—or toxic metals or something,' she added.

'Did you ever hear of any male in this place who suffered from Judy? From all accounts it's to the contrary.'

'Whose accounts?' Laura looked at her sharply.

'Slovenly speech. I mean—you can tell. She's so jolly. She's like you.'

'*What?*'

'I mean, in the fun she gets out of life.'

'You can't have fun at other people's expense.'

'Who's been caught?'

'How d'you mean?'

'Someone's in trouble. Married man? Paternity order? You're not sympathising with Bill Lynch, are you?'

'It's nothing specific. Well, perhaps—when she starts breaking up homes. . . .'

'You said you knew nothing about Olive.'

'Only that she'd left and why. It's enough, isn't it?'

Ruth had the feeling that she was being scrutinised.

'Where do you think Olive is?' she asked.

'Olive? Oh, in Sheffield, I suppose. She comes from there.'

There were noises from upstairs. Laura nodded towards the ceiling.

'Your household's awake. I'm off. I must get someone to mend the fence before another animal goes rampaging through your garden.'

'Come over to lunch tomorrow.'

'Love to. The boys have got something planned with Sue and it's John's day off. Is Emily coming?'

'I'll ask her after breakfast.'

Laura left and shortly afterwards Susan came down, dressed for riding, followed by Paul. They were both grumbling about the continued break in the weather.

There was no sign of Ned and no one commented on his absence. Breakfast was a kind of running buffet at Heathens' Low.

While they were eating, Marilyn Hibbert arrived: a slight pale girl obviously pregnant and looking rather drawn. Ruth observed her closely and wondered when she was going to meet someone in Bardale who didn't look as if they were in trouble. She was starting to feel depressed. It was a grey cold day and not conducive to goodwill but she wished others would make an effort. When Paul and Susan had left the kitchen and Marilyn was washing the dishes, she asked rather sharply:

'Are you feeling all right?'

'A little tired maybe.' The girl smiled wanly.

'You've been doing too much,' Ruth commented, thinking that nevertheless there wasn't much to do in Marilyn's house until the baby came. 'How's Annie?'

'She's fair.'

Ruth regarded the thin shoulders thoughtfully.

'How's Michael?' she pressed, slowly drying a plate.

'He's all right.'

'He likes the new job?'

'It's not so new now, Mrs Stanton.'

'No. I forget I've been away for so long. But he likes working in the quarry?'

'Yes.' The girl turned, pushing away her hair with the back of a wet hand. 'It's a steady job with a good pay packet.' Unspoken between them hung the rider: 'He'd better like it!'

'Do the shifts bother you?'

'No. He's lucky to have a job at all these days. Quarrying's all we've got left here. All those unemployed! It's frightening.'

The girl's mother had abandoned her as a baby; she'd never known a father. Brought up in the comparative

40

warmth and security of a Dr Barnardo's home, she knew about privation and dole queues if only from the knowledge that these were just round the corner if a gear slipped for some reason—like pregnancy when you weren't married, or a window left open at the back of the supermarket.

'People who want a job can get one,' Ruth pointed out. 'It's a matter of being willing to change your occupation and to move around. Sometimes people have to follow the work.'

'Michael's happier in Bardale,' Marilyn said.

Safer, Ruth thought, that's what she means. He would have been taken on at the quarry only through the good offices of his father, who was foreman and had worked there all his life. Joe would have vouched for Michael. And now it was the family keeping him straight, but Marilyn would doubt her ability to do it on her own if they had to leave the dale. In any event, with the labour pool so full, who would employ a man with a prison record? No one so young should be so vulnerable, Ruth thought, glancing at the girl's worn face and imagining Susan in Marilyn's position. Aloud she said:

'You must take more care of yourself. Don't lift anything, and don't do any floors today. They can miss a weekend.'

'I must vacuum, Mrs Stanton.'

'Just down here then. I don't want you carrying that machine upstairs. Besides, with everyone out over the weekend, the floors will be filthy by tonight. I'll get Judy to come in on Monday. You need a rest.'

'Why don't you ask Mum?'

'She's well, is she? That's fine. I will. Now I'm going up to see Miss Jebb.'

Paul joined her and, wearing gum boots and raincoats—it had stopped raining but the grass was soaked

—they followed a path through the woods to the Catcliff property.

They found Emily feeding her hens. She was accompanied by a yellow Labrador bitch and the tortoiseshell queen called Vinya. They admired the dog and the hens, commiserated over the theft of the White Wyandotte, and asked the old lady to Sunday lunch. Emily said she would be delighted. Her beautiful manners failed to hide the fact that she was slightly abstracted. Once or twice Ruth noticed that she glanced towards the drive.

They said goodbye and started down the hill to Bardale. On the way they met Judy Scroop.

She was a well-built girl with a lot of thick black hair, slightly greasy: the kind of hair Italian peasants sell to wig-makers. She had a big red mouth, a smooth skin and friendly eyes. She looked not unlike a film star of the forties as she came striding up the hill, her red overcoat swinging back to reveal the strong young body and a gored skirt ridiculously and unevenly shortened to show the splendid thighs. Happy and colourful, she exuded *Je Reviens*, causing Ruth's eyes to narrow suspiciously. She was Everyman's dream of the compliant country wench.

'Hallo, Miz' Stanton,' she called. ' 'Lo, Mr Trevena.' Her tone softened outrageously.

'Where are you going, Judy?' Ruth asked. They were above the doctor's gate.

'I'm going up to Miss Jebb. She sent for me.'

'*Sent* for you? Who did she send?'

'Joe Hibbert. Last night he came. Said as I was to go to bed early. Sauce, wasn't it?'

'Why?'

Judy misunderstood. 'Mum said so. She's not gentry, Mum said, she's got no call to go ordering us about

42

as if we was in service. What d'you think, Miz' Stanton?'

'Miss Jebb was thinking of your own good, although you look well enough on it—late nights, I mean. Is she spring-cleaning?'

'Spring-cleaning—in October?' She pealed with laughter. 'No. Joe Hibbert, he said I was to go and lend a hand because there was a lot on this weekend with you coming back and all. But then *you'd* want me, wouldn't you, not Miss Jebb? Silly old cow,' she added cheerfully.

'Judy Scroop,' Paul said severely. 'If you're bringing that brood of yours up to be cheeky, I shall report you to the local authority.'

'Mr Renishaw, you mean.' She grinned at him, her eyes on a level. 'You wouldn't report me to no one, Mr Trevena, not you.' Not for the first time Ruth was almost appalled by the curious innocence of the girl, totally unselfconscious in another woman's presence. 'And Mr Renishaw wouldn't hurt me,' she assured him. 'But you got no call to worry 'bout them kids. They be brought up right. Mum's strict, ain't she, Miz' Stanton?'

'She wasn't strict enough for you,' Ruth said firmly.

'Oh, Mum hasn't had much of a life,' Judy conceded. 'She don't really mind me having fun. She's just got to pretend she does, see? Everyone keeps on at her 'bout me an' the kids but we don't do no one no harm, does us? Mum and me, we understand each other—but I never take no one home, never.'

She was unwontedly serious. She glanced from one to the other for reassurance.

'That's thoughtful of you,' Paul said lamely. 'Where do you—er—'

'Why—' Her face lit up again with laughter, her eyes slid past his shoulder, and suddenly the laughter died. 'There's Miss Jebb,' she said. 'She be waiting. If she's come down the drive, she's mad wi' me. I mun go.'

43

'How's the boy friend?' Ruth asked suddenly.

The girl swung round, her eyebrows raised.

'Which one?' she asked politely.

'Oh, skip it.' Ruth turned and they resumed their walk. They were each silent for long enough to know that the encounter had made the other uncommonly thoughtful.

'She's enjoying life,' Paul said at length, carefully, and Ruth recalled with some surprise that she had wondered when she would meet someone in Bardale who wasn't in trouble. Ambiguously, it turned out to be the one person who, almost literally, was always 'in trouble' in country parlance.

'I wonder where she goes,' he speculated.

'Jagger's Barn.'

'How on earth do you know?'

'Emily Jebb says courting couples drive away the barn owls. There's no one of an age to court in the Street except Judy.'

'And?'

'Men from Bull Low, I presume.'

They came to the Bardale road. On their right was the upper bridge and a widening triangle of water meadows, their boundaries formed by the steep slope under Bardale Bank and the river. On their left was the Street and the terrace of houses with the senior Hibberts' cottage nearest to them.

Across the road from this was Joe's garage: an old wooden shelter, green with lichen, and roofed with corrugated iron. It was empty now with the doors propped open by chunks of stone.

Behind the garage were a few trees, and, impending over all, the great bulging cliffs, so close above that the roof of Joe's garage was strewn with small stones.

A beaten and rather squalid-looking path ran along

44

the side of this shelter and ended at the roots of an oak below the cliff. There was a small black opening in the ground. This was one entrance to Styx Hole, the cave system which gave Bardale its only claim to fame.

Paul and Ruth, who were totally uninterested in caving, ignored it, and knocked at the Hibberts' door.

Annie Hibbert was a small square woman with thinning hair and eyes which could once have been rather fine: grey and long-lashed under well-shaped brows, but which now were sunk in deep sockets. It was a curious alliance: the good bone structure of the skull and the dumpy body. She looked as if she took too little exercise and too much food. She was fifty and had lately become obsessed by the thought of her own ill-health.

As she led them to the front room, Ruth said cheerfully and mendaciously:

'You're looking well, Annie.'

The woman glanced at her warily.

'I'm fair,' she said as if she begrudged it. 'But the damp goes for me arthritis. You wouldn't know up there, in Foodale, but even before dark, mist lies up this bottom like a shroud, and it stays till dawn. It do no good shutting windows; it creeps down chimneys.'

'Oh, Annie! It was clear as a bell last night in the Street!'

'It were exception then. Goes for your lungs too—'

'Annie, Marilyn's doing too much. Would you come up instead of her on Monday?'

The woman looked at her shrewdly.

'You seen it too. She'll be all right.'

'But she looks worn out!'

'Bad time,' Annie muttered, straightening a lace runner on the sideboard. 'Waiting—it goes on so long, don't it?' In the cluttered room, shadowed by the huge cliffs,

45

her eyes looked like pits in the pale face. 'I mind carrying our Michael. I thought t'would never end.' She remembered that one of her audience was a man but her tone didn't change. 'Ay,' she said sombrely, staring at Paul. ' 'Tis worse for the man, if he's a good 'un.'

Paul moved uncomfortably. 'So I've heard.'

'Michael will be looking forward to it,' Ruth put in rather wildly.

'Oh, yes. Michael will make a good father.'

She said it with the same confidence vouchsafed by Marilyn when she'd maintained that Michael liked his job. The Hibbert women were pretty managing, but then if the weakest member of the family was easily influenced by bad companions, perhaps his only chance of salvation, or at least of retaining his grip, lay in his women folk being firm.

'And Hibbert's like a dog with two tails,' Annie went on. 'We're a very close family. Never been much for outside.'

'But you're all related in the Street,' Ruth pointed out. 'You were a Raven, and surely Mr Padley's your cousin?'

'No. Padley's Hibbert's relative. He's the youngest son of Hibbert's father's sister.'

Paul tried to look intrigued.

'That makes Padley Hibbert's cousin,' he said.

'That's right.'

'Then everyone in the Street is related, at least by marriage,' Ruth said, trying to remember how this had started.

'A closed community,' Annie commented.

'Bardale?' Ruth asked helpfully.

'The Street, of course.' She remembered her manners. 'Not but what Miss Jebb and your own family is dales folk, and then there's Doctor—' Her face softened surprisingly and the charcoal eyes glowed.

'You don't include the Scroops and the Lynches in your closed community then?' Paul asked mischievously.

Annie looked at him.

'I've got nothing against drink,' she said. A tight smile stretched her face. 'Can I offer you some sherry, Mrs Stanton?'

'No, that's very kind of you, Annie, but we've got a lot to do today. It may not look like it but Mr Trevena's working on an idea for a film.'

'About Bardale?'

'Just an idea,' he admitted, embarrassed.

'Old damp place,' Annie said, but with affection.

'It would make a great film.' Paul grew bolder. 'Those monstrous cliffs and the straight street. Autumn dusks and your terrible mist. Dark things could happen here.' He turned to Ruth.

'Dark things happen,' echoed Annie Hibbert.

They looked at her in inquiry.

'You know something,' Paul said.

'You can feel it.' She hugged her elbows as if she were cold. 'And there's Styx Hole under our feet: miles of passages in the dripping rock. What's happening down there?'

'What could be happening, Annie?' Ruth asked.

Annie stared across the road at Joe's garage.

'Anything,' she said. 'Where's Olive Lynch?'

They walked down the Street, quickly and in silence, past Marilyn's closed house, past Mrs Padley's shop with that door, too, closed against the chill—the sun reached the bottom of the dale only for one short hour on an autumn day, never in winter—past John Eden's surgery.

'She's mad—' Paul started—to be hushed immediately. She gripped his arm by way of emphasis.

47

'It's cold for you, Henry,' she said loudly.

Henry Raven sat in his wheelchair at the open window; above an enormous cocoon of eiderdowns, his white moon face and currant eyes were framed by a scarlet balaclava.

'Don't you start, mum,' he wheezed. 'Lily's doing out kitchen wi' t'Hoover and Ah says Ah'll sit 'ere in me place at t'window and then. Ah'll not 'ave 'er round me legs wi' them old cables. Dangerous, that's what them is.'

'You'll know everything,' Paul accused recklessly. 'Where's Olive Lynch?'

'In Sheffield, where she'm no right to be. Should be back 'ere and send yon randy piece packing.' Simmering noises came from his chest. He was laughing. 'Yo' bin talking too much to Miz' Stanton; it be all murder in 'er mind, not but what we couldn't do wi' a nice juicy killin' in Bardale. Liven things up, wouldn't it?'

'You bloodthirsty old reprobate.' Paul regarded him with admiration. He watched Henry's physical condition deteriorate with every visit he made to the dale but the old man's spirit was indomitable. 'Who would you say will murder whom?'

'Ah,' Henry said cunningly. He thought for a moment, unwilling, even in fun, to relinquish the position of village oracle. 'Ah'll tell yo' when Ah knows—maybe.'

'Do you ever get the appalling feeling,' Paul observed as they proceeded, 'that some chance idea which passed through your mind and you caught by the tail and started to elaborate, that it starts to happen in reality?'

'As if you conceived it, and then it took on an independent life in another dimension and you bore the basic responsibility? That's Frankenstein's monster. Yes. It's terrifying.'

'I won't believe it.' He shook his head violently. 'I take back everything I said about foul play. It's a wicked

48

place in autumn—the Street. And as you said, Annie's neurotic. It's what they euphemistically term her time of life, I suppose. Poor Annie. I could do with a drink.'

They were approaching the Quiet Woman. On their right, beyond the river, which here emerged from behind the houses to flow under the road by way of the bottom bridge, the shabby walls of Hades Flatt were just visible through a straggling belt of alders. They could hear the Scroop children playing, and glimpse small figures through the leaves.

They left the road and approached the inn which, in an effort to attract trade, had been smartened self-consciously. This had been unsuccessful because Bardale, far from holding any attraction for tourists, was intimidating, the lure of Styx Hole being so esoteric that only cavers appreciated it. These, for one of those reasons associated with sporting fashion, at the moment favoured the pub in the next village. Few Bardale people used the Quiet Woman; most of the inhabitants of the council estate at Bull Low patronising the Wild Boar below the quarry.

The Woman, as everyone called it, was long, low, whitewashed, and strung meagrely with fairy lights. Its sign: a headless woman, was newly executed and the artist had been rather too free with the carmine paint where the head should be.

On this dull Saturday the bar was lit and cheerful. Bill Lynch, regarding their approach with an artificial smile and watchful eyes as he polished a glass, was a flawed caricature of mine host.

They greeted him, ordered beer, and arranged themselves on stools, aware suddenly that they had held no preliminary discussion concerning the direction of the conversation. Did one, thought Ruth, ask after a man's wife when she'd discovered him virtually in bed with

49

the village tart, or did one ignore the lady's absence, thus implying that one was party to the scandal?

As they exchanged chit-chat about the comparative merits of Adriatic resorts, she asked herself the question: could Bill Lynch be a murderer? Had he buried his wife in the potato patch or pushed her down Styx Hole?

Chapter 4

SQUADRON LEADER LYNCH had retired from the Royal Air Force some years ago so he would be aged around fifty but his face was plump and unlined, the hair short, straight, and smelling slightly of brilliantine. He spoke with the hint of a London accent which gave him a spuriously contemporary air.

The Lynches were snobs and, what was worse, bores.

Ruth had found Olive Lynch even duller than her husband. She'd favoured tweeds and matching lambswool jumpers, and the fact that Ruth herself always looked elegant and totally unsuitable for Bardale, whether it was in an Yves St Laurent number or a plastic mac, must have seemed like an affront. Since she came to the dale, Olive's brogues had become clumpier, her pearls smaller and her latest acquisition, Ruth recalled now, had been an enormous sheepskin overcoat, picked up at a sale of bankrupt stock last June.

She must have taken it as a personal insult to find Judy Scroop in her bed—well, making it afterwards.

Ruth became aware that the conversation was flagging.

'...has all the advantages without the dirt,' Lynch was saying in her direction.

'Exactly.' She smiled neutrally.

'You managed to get across the frontier?'

She hesitated.

'Albania wasn't in her brief. Our story's concerned only with Yugoslavia,' Paul put in smoothly.

She wondered how long the man could continue without mentioning his wife. The atmosphere was colourless. Feeling mischievous rather than suspicious, she slipped off her stool and glanced at Lynch as she did so. His eyes flickered towards her but without interest. She went through the back and up the stairs to the bedroom floor.

'. . . It's Ruth's concern at this stage,' Paul was saying when she returned. 'I come in later. At the moment I'm interested in Bardale.'

Lynch's slightly protruberant eyes appeared to become more prominent.

'Professionally?'

'In the quarry. An industrial epic.'

'Ah, yes. Expansion, economic growth, full employment. Excellent. What's the theme—or is that it?'

Paul nodded enthusiastically: 'Exciting, isn't it?' He turned to her with sudden decision. 'I'm not going back, my dear. How about some sandwiches with our drinks and we'll go straight on to the quarry? Save time.'

'That's a good idea.' So he'd thought better of his recent avowal to forget the possibility of foul play. 'We can't interrupt Ned at this stage.' She glanced at Lynch, drawing him into a conspiracy to leave genius undisturbed.

'Sandwiches,' Lynch said. 'Certainly. Olive's away and I'm not very handy with the tin opener but Lily Raven will be in at any time; she's looking after me now.' He glanced at the clock above the bar. It said five to one. 'She'll make up something.'

Paul raised his eyebrows.

'Gone separately this year?' he commented jovially

on a rising inflection. 'What part has Mrs Lynch favoured?'

Lynch was expressionless.

'Sheffield.'

'For a *holiday*?'

'She's not on holiday. She's looking after her mother who's broken her thigh.'

'I *am* sorry,' Ruth put in. 'How long will she stay?'

'Well, the old lady's recovering but she's still bed-ridden and even with a home help—you know how it is. She won't go into a nursing home and there's got to be someone with her at night. We're slack now. Olive rings every evening and I've told her to stay there. I can manage. Lily looks after me very well.'

'I'm sure she does,' Ruth murmured. 'If there's anything we can do—'

'That's kind of you, but I promise you, I'm managing perfectly. People,' Lynch said coldly, 'are very helpful in Bardale.'

'I've always found that,' Ruth said.

Paul, feigning horror at the prospect of the afternoon's grind, ordered whisky and pressed Lynch to join him. Ruth stayed on beer. Lily was late and they'd worked through two rounds before she arrived.

She was a small grey sparrow hawk of a woman who looked quite incapable of moving her gross and helpless husband. Wearing an unfortunately funereal combination of mauve frock and black coat, she paused in the bar to receive her orders. Her dark eyes, vital as Henry's but devoid of humour, regarded them stonily.

'There's only cheese,' she told them, 'and there's no brown bread. I can slip up to the shop for an 'Ovis and get some 'am.'

'They even know what you *eat*!' Paul exclaimed with awe when she'd shut the front door again.

'They know everything,' Lynch said, startling Ruth for, where she might have expected him to comment morosely or at least wryly, she realised that he'd uttered the remark with a kind of satisfaction, almost of pride. She looked hard at the man and saw his eyes change. His thin mouth moved and his glance slid over the cream suède blouse that his wife would have considered so unsuitable for Bardale. He was leering.

'She telephones every night,' Paul said reflectively.
'He says so.'
'We've only got his word for any of it. I wonder what Lily knows.'
They were strolling along the pavement that bounded Bull Low: a dull collection of pebble dash houses and wood trim in cardinal colours, of old cars and television aerials and lines of washing.
'The Scotch hadn't the slightest effect on him,' Paul resumed sadly.
'Didn't you notice? He ogled me.'
'I did, but that's in character, wouldn't you say?' He regarded her doubtfully.
'Is it significant in the present context? What is his character? A womaniser, repressed and controlled by Olive, playing while the cat's away, either temporarily or permanently?'
'He's not that much of a mouse. I reckon your lecherous Lynch could be an awkward customer. And there's newly turned earth in the back garden. I saw it from the loo.'
'So did I. He's lifted his potatoes, like I said.'
'Doesn't a potato patch strike you as a little inconsistent with the squadron leader's pretensions?'
'Maybe it's lettuces and things, and he's doing some autumn digging.'

'Overlooked by all the windows of Hades Flatt. Could Brenda be an accomplice?'

She pondered. 'I notice you don't mention Judy.'

'Definitely not. She'd never keep a thing to herself.'

'There's absolutely no reason at all why Brenda should cover up for Lynch. He's a loner if ever I saw one. He's also powerful but is he powerful enough? It would need amazing stamina to dig a grave overnight. Have you ever trenched a garden? You take up one spadeful —the depth of the spade—then you dig a spade's depth below that, and that's only about two feet. Now, if a body's about one foot deep—I mean, if it takes up about twelve inches of depth lying on its back, or front —you'd need, for safety, some extra feet between it and the surface. If you buried your victim the traditional six feet down, you'd have to dig a seven-foot hole. No wonder murder victims are always found in "shallow graves".'

'What d'you mean: "shallow graves"? You don't know about the ones that aren't found.'

They turned left at the entrance to the quarry where a placard in pale blue and black skinned with dust announced BARDALE ROADSTONE LTD. As they climbed the gradient, a film of pale mud deepened to ooze. There was no provision for pedestrians. Paul looked at Ruth's cream pants with admiration.

'You think of everything,' he said. Already their gum boots were plastered with mud. As they ascended, lorries, loaded with hot tarmac and trailing steam, crawled down the incline on their way to the new motorway.

They were expected at the office and she introduced him to the manager: a Jebb, and a distant connection of Emily's. They chatted until Joe Hibbert arrived to supervise the conducted tour. Ruth, who had seen the quarry before and who had no intention of going

55

through it again, said goodbye and, making sure that no shot was about to be fired, left by a rough track which climbed out of the pit on the side away from the village and curved back to run along the top of the face some distance from the edge.

Once she was on top, perversely, she approached the lip to look down on the scene below.

The face was about one hundred and fifty feet high and from where she stood she could see back along it and down, to where mechanical shovels were loading huge lorries, toy-like at this distance, but the crash of rocks on steel plating was appalling. She wondered, not for the first time, about the effect on the drivers' hearing.

When they were loaded, the lorries sped away at a great pace, stopped, reversed till their rear wheels nudged an earth rampart, the back tipped up, and the load slid into the crusher.

From there the scene was all diagonals: of closed chutes or soaring belts bearing the crushed stone. Everything, the roofs of cars outside the distant office, trees in Bardale, grass above the face, was covered with beige dust like fur. Even the jackdaws looked shabby. All the roads inside the quarry were deep in the ubiquitous cream mud.

The face was, curiously, composed of brown limestone with grey and black intrusions—yet the dust was pale. The quarry was a fascinating place. She didn't like it but she found the processes, from the firing of a shot which could bring down thirty thousand tons, to the crusher which fragmented a one-ton boulder in a minute, so stupendous as to be just this side of mystery and the wrong side of horror.

She stared gloomily at the crusher, invisible and cased in its box of hardened steel, then she turned and made for the track which would bring her to the Outlands.

As she walked, the dust decreased and grass started to show green again. Black and white cows grazed on clean pasture and at the top of the far lip of Bardale the occasional oak was turning gold.

It was a glorious afternoon, with blue sky appearing in the west and no one about. She had a bad moment on the Outlands when, with a thud of hooves, a squad of roan bullocks came rushing to look at her, but, knowing that Padley's bull was a biscuit-coloured Charollais, she stood her ground and the beasts stopped short, then with much trampling and tossing of horns, escorted her officiously to the gate at the top of Foodale.

She was never gloomy for long and she was amused and happy as she came down the track, hearing the brook gurgling under the wall and one of Emily's hens announcing the laying of an egg with an hysterical paean of triumph.

Her own drive was untidy and sodden with dead leaves and she sighed. There were no gardeners to be had in Bardale. Emily and Laura struggled gamely with their own acres, but Heathens' Low fared worse. I'm rich, Ruth thought helplessly, regarding the bough of an ash which must have come down while she was abroad; I've got an empty, furnished coach house and there are a million unemployed and I can't find a bloody gardener! It was a pity that Ned's concern for the environment was too far-reaching to cover their own immediate acres.

She went in the side door, saw that the door of his study, the first on the left, was shut, and continued quietly along the passage, glancing idly in other rooms as she passed. The house seemed empty. There was only one used plate and a knife on the draining board in the kitchen. She breathed a sigh of relief. A man who cooked but didn't clear up, and a young girl in a hurry could wreak havoc after the help had left.

It was not yet four o'clock. She kicked off her gum boots, padded to the dining room and poured herself a sherry. She sipped it, looking out of the window.

The terrace of Heathens' Low, paved with stone slabs and set with stonecrop and saxifrage, was broad and faced south. They looked across the tiny ravine of Foodale to the Outlands. The roof of Jagger's Barn showed above the solid wall of its yard. Below the terrace birches were lemon and silver in the light. She regarded her domain fondly and with deep satisfaction, smiled to herself, and turned—to find Ned watching her from the doorway.

'Don't do that too often,' she said after a tense pause. 'I thought the house was empty.'

'Did I startle you? Sorry.' He looked round vaguely. 'Where's Paul?'

'Joe's taking him round the quarry. You look a little lost, darling; come in and have a sherry. How are the Jebbs?'

'The Jebbs?'

'Your book.'

'Ah, the Jebbs! I haven't touched the book for weeks.'

'I got the impression you were immersed in it.'

'I don't know what could have made you think that.'

'When I was in Slovenia,' she said firmly, 'I rang you from Ljubljana and I felt quite sure you were absorbed. You must remember: I intended coming back in the middle of September. You rather put me off, implied you were—you wouldn't welcome distractions at that moment. So I stayed away another two weeks.'

'It was nothing.'

'But—' She paused. 'Why did I get the impression you were in trouble?' she asked herself thoughtfully.

58

'I wasn't in trouble.' He gave a bark of laughter.

She rose from the sofa and walked to the sideboard. Absently but very carefully she poured herself a sherry, standing with her back towards him. To her astonishment she realised that she was hot with anger.

'I remember now,' he exclaimed. 'There's going to be a big public inquiry about proposals to flood Conies Dale. A protection committee's been set up and they've asked me to help collect evidence. That's right. Hell of a job. I had to go through all my files and to correlate information from all over: Wales, Dartmoor, the Lake District, even Scotland. Yes, you must have phoned right when I was in the middle of it. I was overworked. I'm sorry.'

'You should have explained.'

'There are two motors of three hundred horsepower each and they revolve at nine hundred and sixty revs a minute. Its technical term is an impact breaker.'

Paul took a sip of his wine and regarded them solemnly.

'I think it's totally obscene,' he said with relish.

'Why?' Susan asked.

'Nothing outside an act of God has a right to be so powerful that it can smash a boulder to atoms in a few seconds. I applaud thunderbolts. I deplore the impact breaker. And what is its purpose? To enable your mother to reach home slightly faster in her ostentatious motor car.'

'It's no more ostentatious than your Bentley,' Susan pointed out. 'And road metal is only one of the products. They put the stuff in face powder and toothpaste and flour.'

'Not the flour we use,' Ruth protested, roused from a reverie which was less a matter of dreaming than of sensual delight in the atmosphere of her dining room.

The light over the table was of low capacity and shielded by a parchment shade round which the bulls of Lascaux swayed on elegant hooves. The huge circular table had no pedigree but it had solidity and a warm sheen. They were at that stage of the meal where they'd finished eating but had not yet thought of coffee. The men had been on their best behaviour. Susan, deceptively mature this evening in a long green dress, showed unmistakable signs of the beauty she would be in a few years' time, and Ruth herself, in blue velvet, felt rich and cherished and at peace with the world.

'Will it make a film?' she asked, watching the plummy lights caught in her Chateauneuf.

'Oh yes,' Paul said firmly. 'It will make a great documentary.'

'What are you doing it for?' Ned asked.

'Independent. I've quarrelled with the BBC.'

'I mean, why are you doing it?'

'I see.' Paul pondered, shooting a glance at Ruth. 'It has relevance to the modern world,' he said meaninglessly; both he and Ned had drunk a good deal of wine.

'What hasn't?' His host was rhetorical.

'Michael's on the crusher.' Paul turned to Ruth.

'Michael Hibbert? I thought he was a lorry driver.'

'Euclids, they call them. Magnificent, isn't it? Who but an industrialist would dream of naming a lorry after a Greek mathematician?'

'It's a very responsible job,' Ned told him.

'Driving a Euclid? Does one say "*an* Euclid", I wonder?'

'Operating the crusher.'

'Quite. Did you know they have to get down on the apron if there's a blockage and break the jam, as it were, with crowbars?'

60

'They stop the apron,' Ruth assured him. 'It's on a different system from the crusher.'

'They don't—'

'They don't, Mum.' Ned and his daughter spoke together.

'Joe only just escaped once,' Ned elaborated. 'He thought a boulder was being held back, but it moved. He managed to jump clear—just.'

'Nine hundred and sixty revs a minute,' Paul breathed. 'And those ghastly kilns with the tiny peep hole and a pinprick of orange fire at the end! Thank God everything's automatic; I couldn't bear the thought of those processes being manual. The place terrifies me as it is.'

'The crusher's manual,' Susan pointed out.

'Oh no, ducky. The crusher is a monstrous *machine*. Poor Michael isn't a *man*; he's the crusher attendant. That's the technical term, would you believe it?'

'You have enjoyed yourself,' Ruth said, smiling.

He realised he had been monopolising the conversation.

'Have you had a good day?' he asked Ned politely.

Ned excused himself early on the grounds that he was working on the incidence of bowel cancer in areas with fluoridated water supplies. Susan went to bed leaving Paul and Ruth to discuss the Balkan script. Time passed quickly and it was midnight before they started to feel tired.

There was a light under the study door when they went up but Ruth didn't go in to say goodnight.

When she'd undressed she put out her light and opened the window. It was dark but subconsciously she took in the study light down on her left. It was mild and dry and quite clear. She heard a fox bark from the

Catcliff. The pong's not bothering us.'

He went to the sitting room with the Sunday papers. Then Ruth discovered that the bottle of Emily's favourite sherry was nearly empty and he was sent away in Ned's Mini to try to find more at the Woman or the Wild Boar.

The Edens arrived and hung their raincoats in the passage and changed to shoes. Everyone wore gum boots in Bardale in the autumn. In the winter it would be snow or walking boots but now it was knee-length rubber.

The women complimented each other on their clothes and Ruth turned to John Eden. She liked him and her pleasure in his company was genuine.

The doctor was shy and honest. He hesitated before he spoke, thinking carefully. He never gave offence socially because people knew what he was about, nor did he offend his patients in the Street. He was totally without pretensions and they respected him. He was a good doctor and, although he never criticised people or even institutions (not in the Street anyway) Bardale knew he was on their side. He had a sharp awareness of human frailties. His patients loved or respected him, usually both. Some feared him. His friends in Foodale felt these emotions too, in a lesser degree. Not the fear, of course; they just liked to have him around, and they never thought the pauses before he spoke, overlong.

He sipped sherry appreciatively, his long and deeply lined face intent on Ruth's account of Yugoslavia. Ned came in, licking his fingers, distressed about the consistency of strawberry pulp, worrying that chopped walnuts might not blend. Laura suggested almonds and he went out again, beaming.

Emily arrived wearing a severe navy coat and skirt and a cameo in lace at her throat. She looked very nice but her face was a trifle haggard. She explained that she'd had no sleep last night because a fox had been barking up near the hens. She'd been out several times to drive it away.

'I hope I didn't wake you,' she said apologetically to Ruth. 'But you sleep at the other end of the house.'

'I heard the foxes. Ned was out too—' There was a gasp behind her. He had returned and was staring at her in astonishment. She faltered, then smiled at him. 'There was I thinking all the world was asleep except Ned trying to glean inspiration in the woods and, of course, me, and it seems the whole of Foodale was actively pursuing its interests, not to mention the foxes.'

She turned to the Edens, including them.

'Yes,' John admitted after his usual pause. 'I was out too. Dora Bagshawe at Paradise Farm had her third and I didn't get home till about one.'

'Not me!' Laura laughed. 'I went to bed at ten with a horror called *Blood on my Mind*. I remember opening it, and that was that. Off like a log. Didn't even know John had come to bed.'

A Mini was heard coming up the drive.

'At last,' Ruth said darkly. 'Why is it that always when you send a man away from a party, he takes such a perishable long time performing an errand? Is one's house so objectionable?'

Paul came in bubbling with excitement. He thrust a bottle at Ruth, changed his mind, said, 'I'll open it,' but turned to the company, perfunctorily acknowledging greetings, hugging the bottle.

'Another disappearance!' he announced.

'Who?' Several people spoke.

'Judy Scroop.'

There was dead silence, then:

'Since when?' This was Ned.

'She didn't come home last night.'

Again no one spoke. He looked round the circle. He hadn't been prepared for this. He turned to Ruth.

'Not a common occurrence?' he asked, almost timidly.

'No,' she said heavily. 'Judy's a good mother.'

Paul's eyebrows shot up.

'She never stays out all night,' Laura elaborated. 'Who told you this?' she asked curiously.

'Brenda came in the Woman while I was buying the sherry and having a beer with Lynch. She was practically hysterical—in a quiet way. Huge eyes staring at you, pinning you down; you know Brenda. She was asking us where Judy was—as if we'd know. Distraught, that's the word. I'd love to have that woman in a close-up of a crowd of peasants: women waiting at the pit head after an accident down the mine: sharp faces with their souls in their eyes. She looked desperately incongruous wearing that coat.'

'Coat?' Ruth repeated.

'Enormous sheepskin thing, down to her knees.'

'But that's—!' Ruth turned to Laura, to Emily Jebb.

'That's what?' He was sharp as a ferret. 'What's odd about Brenda's coat? It was never yours so she didn't get it from you.' He stared at Ruth doubtfully, then dismissed the thought of her in a sheepskin overcoat. 'Where did she get it?'

No one answered him. Their faces were blank but behind the lack of expression they were thinking hard. Even Ruth was rejecting him.

It was Emily who spoke first and they all turned to her.

'It's Olive Lynch's coat,' she said gently. 'I should say, it *was* her coat. She has obviously given it to one of the Scroops.'

'That coat was new,' Laura said in disbelief.

66

'It was terribly hot and heavy,' John Eden pointed out. 'Probably she disliked it as soon as she wore it. A hampering thing.'

No one commented on this. It was curious that six intelligent people who were in the habit of conversing on virtually any subject, could find nothing to say about Mrs Scroop wearing Mrs Lynch's coat, not to mention the disappearance of a village character. Of course, when they realised that they were behaving oddly, they started to talk.

'She's nipped off to Sheffield and missed a lift back,' Ruth said.

'Olive?' Paul asked, confused.

'Judy Scroop.'

'That seems most likely,' Emily agreed. 'Last night was Saturday and she likes dancing very much. There will be several dances in Sheffield on a Saturday evening.'

'When did she leave *you*?' Ruth asked.

Emily looked thoughtful.

'I think she went home about five.'

'Brenda was saying that Judy came in for tea and left at seven,' Paul told them.

John Eden and Ned said nothing.

'Who was she going to meet?' Ruth asked. 'Did Brenda know?'

'I don't know if she *knew*. She didn't say.'

'Funny.' Ruth's eyes met Laura's. 'Goodness,' she exclaimed. 'How parochial can you get? Here am I, gossiping like—like—' She tried to think who epitomised gossip in Bardale.

'Olive Lynch?' Paul suggested.

There was another of those long silences.

'This is good sherry,' Emily said judiciously. 'It isn't your usual brand, Ruth, but I like it. What is it?'

* * *

'You could have cut the atmosphere with a knife,' Ruth said. 'What's going on? Where is she?'

It was four o'clock. The luncheon guests had gone, Ned was working, and Susan was in a hot bath. She had come home drenched and filthy after getting Padley's bullocks back to the Outlands. Someone had left the gates open at Jagger's Barn and the beasts had got in the woods. Ruth had just come down and joined Paul in the sitting room.

She sank down gracefully on the hearth rug, the folds of her dress arranging themselves like a frame. The room was dim and cosy with one table lamp lit and a good fire in the grate.

'How would I know?' He shared her bewilderment. The undercurrents were powerful, weren't they? Actually, I thought you were with them. I imagined I was the outsider.'

'That was the sheepskin coat,' she told him. 'I was puzzled about it. I still am. Olive was awfully careful about money and although she bought the coat in a sale, it must have cost well over thirty pounds. She only bought it last June. She could scarcely have worn it. It's nasty, isn't it?' She stared at him with big eyes.

'You mean—?'

She looked at the fire as if for reassurance.

'I don't like it,' she murmured.

'I didn't like it yesterday morning, when Annie got all doom-laden about Styx Hole. *Then* it was Olive Lynch. Good God, this is another one!'

'But hadn't you realised that?'

She searched his face. They were both appalled.

'It isn't just—' She stopped. Outside the door the telephone was warbling softly. 'Excuse me.' She rose and went out. She closed the door behind her and this astonished him. He didn't pick up a paper but studied

68

the flames, frowning. She was gone some time.

'Emily.' She explained when she came back. 'She's got some dead leaves blocking a gutter and wants Ned to give her a hand in clearing them.'

'You closed the door,' he said in accusation.

'What?'

'Closed the door. You've never shut me out of a telephone conversation before.'

She sat on the floor again and started to laugh. His face changed: angry, frightened, decisive. He lifted his arm. She stopped laughing. He had been going to hit her.

'I'm not hysterical,' she said quietly.

'I'm sorry. I'm most terribly sorry. What on earth's happening to us?'

'It's not just you and I. We're affected, but it's much bigger, more extensive. Ned will know,' she added, starting to rise, then she remembered that he had gone to Catcliff. 'We'll ask him as soon as he comes back. Ned knows everything that's going on, being one of them.'

'There's a first time for everything,' Police Constable Albert Renishaw said comfortably. 'She's twenty-five and she's not going to stay a girl all her life. You got to expect her to change.'

'People get more responsible with age,' Brenda Scroop said. 'Not less.'

It was growing dark in the public bar and Renishaw looked at his surroundings with faint disapproval. He was a large man, not unhealthy-looking but ponderous. In his mid-forties, he was a good country constable but, having no ambition, he would never be anything more than that: However, he had a lot of shrewd common sense and, if he found the surroundings incongruous, he could justify them. There had been nowhere else

69

available. Brenda had telephoned him at Bull Low but she'd refused to leave the children. They were now in the cottage in the charge of the eldest girl: a precocious nine year old. The offer of the bar had come from Lynch who had retired to his sitting room.

A brandy glass stood in front of Brenda. Now and again she lifted it and tasted the contents. She was a slight woman of about the same age as Renishaw, with dull straight hair worn to her shoulders and the beautiful tragic eyes remarked by Paul Trevena. The fire was banked ready for the evening and gave out no warmth. She wore the sheepskin coat but she still looked cold.

'People alter as they mature.' Renishaw returned to his theme. 'Suppose now she was thinking of settling down—getting married. She'd want to spend some time with the chap, wouldn't she? A weekend, like?'

'She'd tell me,' Brenda said flatly.

'Sure? You mightn't like it.'

'It would be all right if she was serious.'

Neither was aware of anything ridiculous in Brenda's disapproval of her daughter spending a frivolous weekend with a man.

Renishaw sat stolidly in the waning light. He was in uniform, his helmet on the table. It was very still. They could hear the clock ticking above the bar.

'I wouldn't have told you if I wasn't worried,' Brenda said.

'She's only been gone a day.'

'Near twenty-four hours.'

'Well,' he capitulated. 'What do you want me to do?'

'You ask Bill Lynch who she left with. He won't tell me.'

Renishaw studied her.

'It's not official,' he said. 'I don't want to make it

70

official for your sake. You don't want me reporting it to H.Q. and them sending a sergeant down and taking particulars, do you?'

'I don't mind. Why should I?'

'Judy could mind. Chap who's with her would mind, wouldn't he? Suppose he's married? You can't do that, girl.'

'That's his fault—if he's married. He should have thought of that, keeping her out all night. See, she could have phoned me. Bill Lynch would have brought the message across. No, she'd phone me if she could.'

'Well, maybe.... Perhaps she's had a slight accident. Lost her memory.' He had a soft spot for the Scroops. They were no trouble and he was sorry for Brenda. What a girl Judy was to have for a daughter!

'If she's in hospital that's your job to find out—isn't it?' She was doubtful.

'I'll do it. But then it becomes official, see?'

'Try Bill Lynch then.'

Renishaw rose and went carefully through the back.

'Last door on the right at the end of the passage,' Brenda called.

He knocked and Lynch opened the door. The sitting room seemed glaringly lit after the dark bar.

'Mrs Scroop is that worried, sir,' Renishaw began, feeling his way.

'Can I help?' Lynch was affable but serious.

'She'd like to know about Judy. As the girl came here last night, you saw her after her mother did—'

'I don't think I can help much—'

Brenda appeared silently behind Renishaw. Lynch stood aside:

'Come in, Brenda—both of you. Sit down and let's see what we can thrash out between us. Now what d'you want to know?'

71

'Who did she leave with?' Brenda asked, sitting on the edge of a sofa.

'No one,' Lynch said. 'She went out on her own.'

'When did she leave, sir?' Renishaw asked.

'About closing time. I was wondering if she was going to order another drink and how to refuse—and suddenly she looked at the clock, said goodnight and walked out.'

'She didn't go alone,' Brenda said.

'But—' Lynch paused. Her face was hard and her thin mouth set like a trap.

'Could she have joined someone outside?' the constable asked smoothly, aware of the tension. 'Someone who went out first and waited, or who followed her out?'

'She was the last person to go. It was a slack night. Boxing on television, d'you see. And the last people to leave before her were three lads from Bull Low. They left together in some kind of hot rod. You know the thing: it's got a musical horn. They sounded it as they drove away. That was some time before Judy went.'

'Hughie Blount's got a horn like that,' Renishaw said.

Brenda frowned.

'It's not much good, is it?' Lynch glanced at a magazine which lay open on the table. He wanted them to go but in the circumstances he was wary of giving an obvious dismissal. He had enough experience to know that, faced with certain situations, the reactions of middle-aged women were an unknown quantity. Renishaw, living on a housing estate, was braver. He stood up and looked at Brenda.

'I'll get home,' he said, 'and ring the hospitals. But if she's in hospital, she's being looked after. You got no cause for worry there.'

'Suppose she was very ill? Suppose she needed me?'

She rose slowly, staring at Lynch. Her face changed.

'You can't help then, Mr Lynch,' she said coldly.

'No, Brenda, I've told you everything I know, I'm afraid.' He didn't look at her.

She made no move to leave. She licked her lips and swallowed. Renishaw reached out and opened the door. He put his other arm across her shoulders and propelled her out of the room. He looked back at Lynch but it wasn't a conspiratorial look. The publican, catching his eye, shifted uncomfortably.

'Yes, well, I'll see you out.' He stayed sitting, however.

'You stay there,' Renishaw told him. 'I'll let us out.'

'You go back to the kids,' he said, steering her round the side of the inn towards the cottage. 'I'll ring you up if I hear anything. I mean, I'll ring *him*. He'll give you the message.'

'You think so?'

'Come off it, girl. What'you thinking of?'

'His wife's disappeared. Did you know that?'

'I know she's in Sheffield, looking after her old mum.'

'You know the address?'

'No.'

'Find out and go there.'

'Why?'

'Because I reckon you won't find Olive Lynch there, nor ever has been.'

'What are you driving at?'

They were standing near the alders on the river bank, screened from both inn and cottage by the dusk and the trees. A blue light showed in a groundfloor window of Hades Flatt where the children were watching television. The river rushed below them in spate, not loud

73

because there was no fall here, but very powerful.

'See this coat?'

'Of course. I been looking at it.'

'It's hers.'

'Who?'

'Olive Lynch.'

'How do you come by it?'

'He gave it to Judy.'

'How could it be Olive Lynch's then?'

'I don't mean he *bought* it and gave it her. It was Olive Lynch's that she left behind when she disappeared. So he gave it Judy. Cost thirty-three pound. Would he do that if his wife was coming back?'

'How long ago did he give it to Judy?'

'Last week sometime.'

'And when did his wife go?'

She thought carefully.

'Weeks ago,' she said. 'Start of September.'

He looked across the piece of waste ground to the Woman.

'What are you going to do?' she asked.

'I don't know, girl. You go in now. I'm going home. It's my day off tomorrow,' he added with seeming inconsequence.

'You going to Sheffield?'

'I might. I'll come and see you again tomorrow. Let you know what I've found out. What was she wearing —Judy?'

'Her red coat from Paris, what Mrs Stanton give her, green shoes and a green sweater and brown skirt.'

'Handbag?'

'No, she never used one.'

'Carrying anything? No little case or one of those shoulder bags with an airline or initials on the front?'

74

'When did she ever go on an aeroplane? Oh, I see, someone could have given her one. No, she wasn't carrying anything. Never did.'

PART II

Chapter 6

THERE WAS A blotter on Renishaw's desk which he liked to use as a pad when he was writing. In the middle of it lay a lipstick: the case a little dirty but with a stamp of elegance upon it.

'Dior,' the man sitting behind the desk said quietly. 'French. Very classy.' He looked at the younger man on the other side of the desk.

'Smells expensive,' his colleague agreed. The three men continued to stare at it, wondering about its history.

Renishaw, in an old sports jacket and gum boots, said:

'There's not more than two women in Bardale would use something like that.'

'Who?'

'The doctor's wife and Mrs Stanton. She's an authoress.'

'You must tell us about them,' the inspector said but made no move to follow it up.

It was one-thirty on the Monday afternoon. There were sandwich plates and used cups on a tray on the window sill. Outside in the drive a discreet black Cortina stood behind the constable's Mini.

The detectives had been in Bull Low for the better part of an hour but no one was quite sure why they were there. There was a host of minor incidents, nothing sinister on its own, but odd when glimpsed vaguely as a pattern—quite odd—and these had culminated, if you could call it that, in Renishaw's discovery that morning. They looked at the little gilt case on the blotter, each going back over the story the local man had told.

As a policeman he knew the vulnerability of girls like Judy Scroop and he'd been more worried than he would admit to Brenda so, as soon as it was light this morning, he'd taken his shot gun and his Jack Russell terrier and approached Jagger's Barn by the back way, not the path from the Quiet Woman. That is, by way of the track that led from the quarry and across the Outlands.

He'd found the barn empty: closed, empty even of hay, and trampled to a kind of dry morass. The bullocks had been inside and, apart from the yard being wetter, there was little difference between the mud outside and the filthy condition of the barn. No courting couples had ever used it in that state.

He'd gone through the little gate at the top of the green path and started down through the woods. The path was no longer green because the cattle had been here too, cutting up the grass with their hooves and leaving cow pats on the track. He'd gone slowly because the way was steep and, with rocks below, it was dangerous in gum boots. The terrier had been ranging about looking for rabbits and he hadn't seen the actual place where the dog found the lipstick but the animal didn't go far; it must have been close to the path.

He'd come back to Bull Low to find the uniformed sergeant from Hernstone waiting for him. Hernstone was the local market town. He'd come as a result of Renishaw's phoning the hospitals the night before. The sergeant heard the whole story and looked at the lipstick—and gave up. Two women disappeared, the coat belonging to the first being worn by the mother of the second, Judy and Lynch's affair, the lipstick near the girl's stamping ground.... The problem was passed to headquarters and the detectives arrived about twelve-thirty.

Detective-Inspector Andrew Neill was a big-boned man with a Glasgow accent. His hair was thin and pale, receding from a high forehead. His eyes were veiled most of the time by heavy lids which, with deep pouches underneath, reinforced a melancholy stare that made Renishaw fidget. Neill looked old, close to retirement: an old horse about to be pensioned off. He was sallow and he wore a city suit: a man who appeared to have little time and no inclination for the countryside.

Detective-Sergeant Quinney, on the other hand, had a healthy tan and he was young and muscular. He'd followed the story intelligently and without question. Renishaw guessed that the man wasn't unfamiliar with the dales.

Neill stirred and lit a cigarette. He was a heavy smoker.

'If we're down here for anything,' he said, 'it's to look for a missing girl. We've got nothing concrete except that,' he gestured at the lipstick with his cigarette. 'And an expensive coat that seems to belong to too many people. It looks like coincidences, doesn't it? The lipstick isn't the girl's; she'd use something from Woolworth's, but this particular lipstick, which is probably nothing to do with Judy Scroop, is found near her stamping ground. Coincidence? Then there's the coat. If it was an old cloth coat now, no one would think twice about it, but a new sheepskin must have cost a packet. Everything's slightly off-key. And again, no one would think twice if the girl was in the habit of staying out all night, or if she hadn't been the last person to leave the pub.... You checked those lads who left before her?'

'Didn't know she lived in Derbyshire though. Go on,' he said sternly to Renishaw. 'Outdoor woman?'

'Not enthusiastic. Not like Miss Jebb now; she watches birds and makes records for nature societies and such. She's always out; goes everywhere: up among the cliffs even, in the woods, along the tops. You never know where you'll meet Miss Jebb, and interested in everything! Knows more 'n I do about beasts and plants. But Mrs Stanton, if you meet her out, she's charging along swinging her arms and beaming at you, or else she's dawdling in a daydream. She just takes exercise or wanders out to think better, I'd say.'

'Which would she be doing near Spot X?'

'Eh? Oh, I get you. It's a nasty steep old bit, that path. No, she wouldn't take exercise there—unless, of course, she was up in the Outlands and went down to investigate something. . . .'

'Or went up to meet someone?' Neill put in slyly.

'Mrs Stanton? Meeting someone—in Jagger's! You're—'

He stopped in confusion. He'd been about to say that the inspector was mad. They knew it and looked at him with renewed interest.

'It's always the unlikely ones,' Quinney said. 'Pull the wool over your eyes.'

'Not Mrs Stanton,' Renishaw said firmly. 'She's a very smart lady—and I mean "lady". I'm not saying she's any better than she ought to be, but she's got her own flat in London and she's wealthy. If she has a man she'll be one for the trimmings: night clubs and wine—' He paused, out of his depth, and tried again: 'She gets her clothes in Paris, the wife says. I mean, she's just come home in this kind of battledress in white leather stuff—suède, that's it. The wife said it cost a hundred and fifty pound. See? Mrs Stanton, she can choose who she wants

84

and name the place. She's got no call to go to Jagger's Barn.'

'How near was the lipstick to the barn?' Neill asked.

Renishaw gaped at him.

'Less than a hundred yards,' he muttered.

The detectives looked at each other.

'You can't interview a lady because you've found a lipstick that might be hers in a wood.' Neill emphasised the 'lady' slightly.

'Judy Scroop worked for her,' Renishaw pointed out.

'Ha. Working for her Saturday?'

'No. She was with Miss Jebb Saturday. She's next door to the Stantons.'

'You said this Miss Jebb got about,' Quinney reminded him. 'Would it be her lipstick?'

Renishaw chuckled, then thought better of it. 'No,' he said. 'It's not Miss Jebb's.'

'All the same,' Neill said, 'if she gets around a lot, we've an excuse to call on her. We'll see the mother first, and then the publican. We don't need excuses there. We have every reason to interview the people who were most intimate with her.' His mouth assumed a curious shape, the upper lip lifting at one corner to expose a canine tooth so pointed it might have been filed. The constable stared, fascinated.

'I imagine,' Neill said coolly, 'there are going to be quite a number of those. Make a list.'

He appeared to be grinning.

Brenda was frightened less by the detectives than by the apparent seriousness of a situation which warranted their visit. Reluctantly and primly she confirmed Judy's being found in the Lynch bedroom but insisted that the girl was making the bed. Since this seemed by now to be the truth (if not the whole of it) there was no reason to question it. But when she came to the part about Olive going to Sheffield, she took the offensive.

'It's all what he says,' she told them. 'And so it is about my girl being last to leave the pub. When those lads from the estate had gone, there was only her and him left inside. He says she left.' She turned from Neill to Quinney. 'Only *he* says it,' she repeated.

'Is there any reason for him to be frightened of Judy?' Neill asked gently.

Brenda looked away. Her fingers crept up and played round her lips.

'Anything you could tell us would help,' Quinney said. He had a pleasant voice. She looked at him doubtfully.

'A lovely girl, Mr Renishaw says,' he went on. 'Very popular in the village.'

'She's got any number of friends,' Brenda agreed with pride. 'I don't always approve, mind, but she's a sensible girl. All her friends—I mean her real friends, are respectable. Come in and mend things. If ever I want a shelf put up or a bit of garden dug or a fence mended, I've only got to say the word and Judy fetches someone along.'

'But you don't approve of all her friends?'

'No.'

'Like Bill Lynch.'

'He isn't a friend.'

'If she was in trouble—'

'She wasn't,' Brenda said automatically and without heat.

'—and Lynch was the father, would she want him to marry her?'

It was a dim day and the light wasn't switched on. They couldn't see her face until she raised it towards them. It was like a mask.

'I've thought all round it,' she said intensely. 'I've

86

gone over and over what she said these last few days—'
She paused. It was very quiet in the room; they could
hear the river through the closed window. It occurred
to Quinney that she must have packed the younger children off somewhere. 'Either he's got rid of his wife,' she
went on, 'and my girl comes to him and says he's got her
in trouble and what's he going to do about it, or Olive
Lynch went away of her own accord, in a temper like,
and he's afraid she'll come back.... Only thing is—' she
faltered, 'Judy never approached no one like that in her
life. She doesn't want to be married, see? She likes being
free. Tell you the truth, there are six kids, and she
don't know the father of one of 'em, and she don't
care!'

'I've never heard such bloody nonsense in my life.'
Lynch glared at them. ' "Locked in the toilet"! Good
God, everyone locks the toilet! You've been listening
to gossip, probably talking to the cleaner. Of all the
unmitigated claptrap.... That class will make a scandal
out of anything. My wife comes home and the girl and
I just happen to be on the same floor at the same time.
She's attending to her duties and I'm in the toilet, so
Lily Raven tells the world we're having an affair. You
should have approached me in the first instance, you're
well aware of that. I know the chief constable. You're
going to hear more of this.'

'This sheepskin coat of Mrs Scroop's,' Neill said
calmly, as if Lynch hadn't spoken. 'Didn't Mrs Lynch
have a sheepskin coat?'

The publican leaned back in his chair and pursed his
mouth. He looked out of the sitting room window at the
yard. Neill and Quinney waited.

'My wife never liked that coat,' Lynch remarked with
an abrupt change of tone. 'She said she wished she'd

87

never bought the thing; she'd thought it was a bargain at the time. She wanted to get rid of it.'

'I see.' Neill was polite.

'We don't pay the cleaning women much. Can't afford it. They're hard workers though.' Lynch glanced at Neill to see if he understood domestic problems. The inspector nodded sympathetically and sighed. 'I have to watch my expenditure,' Lynch went on. 'My wife comes of a good family and is used to a rather different standard of living.' He looked round the room with distaste and stopped talking.

'She bought the coat,' Neill prompted.

'Yes, of course.' The man's neck was flushed, and he was breathing quickly. 'Fact is,' he said, 'I was annoyed. It was bought with my money, you know: joint account. We had words about it and she took off for her mother's and I gave the damn thing to the cleaner. It was my money,' he repeated belligerently. 'I can do what I like with it—and the girl's a good worker.'

'Quite,' Neill agreed, man to man. 'When is Mrs Lynch returning?'

'She hasn't said.'

'Oh, you're in contact?'

'She telephones, yes.'

'She can do that? I understood she couldn't leave her mother who was bed-ridden.'

'My mother-in-law has the telephone,' Lynch said stiffly.

'Can we have the number?'

'What?'

'Your mother-in-law's telephone number. I want to speak to your wife.'

'She won't be in.'

'She can't leave her mother for long. Just give Sergeant Quinney the number.'

Quinney waited like an eager dog, his pen poised.

Lynch stood up. He was still breathing fast. He gave his head an odd little shake and blinked.

'We'll have a drink,' he said, and moved towards the door.

Neill nodded to the sergeant who followed the publican. The inspector waited, untroubled, listening to the sounds from the bar. His tired eyes strayed to the window. There was an iron gate at the other side of the yard with what must be the vegetable garden beyond. He was still staring at the gate when Lynch returned with a tray bearing three glasses and a bottle of brandy.

'Not for us,' Neill said.

The man feigned surprise, shrugged and poured himself a good measure. He sat down and gulped it.

'What's wrong?' Neill asked.

Lynch was sweating profusely. He looked sick and without subterfuge.

'Nothing. I feel a bit odd now and again lately. Too much weight, I suppose. I'll have to get more exercise, take up squash again.'

'What does your doctor say?'

'Haven't consulted him, old man. I'll be all right. What was the question?'

Neill looked out of the window.

'We were leading up to the whereabouts of your wife.'

'Yes.' Lynch poured some more brandy, not stinting it, and rolled the glass in his hands. He gave a heavy sigh.

'She's with a boy friend in Yorkshire,' he said.

Neill nodded.

'The telephone number?'

'I don't know it, old man.'

'The address?'

'Nor that.'

'Perhaps you know the name of the man?'

'Not his complete name.' Lynch's face assumed a most curious expression. 'Donald,' he said. 'A retired farmer, very comfortably off, breeds racehorses. He's a widower and lives in the North Riding. Got a handle: Sir Donald something.' He was elaborately casual.

'Why did she leave?'

'I suppose because he could offer her a better life. She wasn't cut out to be the wife of a publican.'

'Was she promiscuous?'

'Certainly not!' He was indignant.

'There's this man—'

'Well, she said she was going to run his house, d'you see; that's what she *said*, but I know better. My wife wasn't all she appeared to be on the surface, but she never made an exhibition of herself in public.'

Neill's eyebrows lifted a fraction.

'Did the business with the Scroop girl have any bearing on your wife's decision to leave?'

'Oh yes. Olive wanted a divorce and alimony. She'd think she'd stand a better chance if she caught me with a girl.' He was becoming quite perky. 'She's got a witness too—a neighbour, Lily Raven. I wouldn't be surprised if it was a put-up job.'

'We'll find her quite soon,' Neill said as if the man had asked them to do so.

'That's your problem,' Lynch said coolly. He'd drunk the second brandy and had himself well in hand now.

'It won't be any problem. People can't disappear without any trace. Take Judy Scroop. Someone saw her after she left here at closing time on Saturday evening.'

'I don't doubt it. Judy never went anywhere alone.'

'What's your opinion?'

'Obvious, isn't it? She hitched a lift. There were

90

dances in Hernstone and Sheffield. Some passing motorist picked her up.'

Sitting in the car outside the Quiet Woman Quinney said:

'There's turned earth in his garden.'

'Oh yes.'

'But there is in most people's gardens at the back-end. Why didn't you ask him more about the girl?'

'His condition.'

'What's wrong with him? Heart?'

'That, or blood pressure. Brandy don't help.'

'So you don't think he did it?'

'Come off it, lad. How do I know?' Quinney said nothing. 'All right,' Neill admitted grudgingly. 'It could be him. Motive? The desire to be thought respectable? But he'd been caught virtually in the act by two witnesses and he didn't seem to me to be ashamed of himself. From all accounts she was a sexy piece, and young at that. So he wouldn't kill to cover up a roll in the hay with her. His wife knew, so he didn't have to kill to stop her finding out. His wife,' Neill mused. 'No reason to think he's lying there; told lies in the first place because he was humiliated by his wife running off with another chap but still takes a bit of pride in the fact that the boy friend's a Sir.' His eyes became mournful again: 'Pregnant?'

'Who?' Quinney asked, startled.

'Judy. But he's been around—and in the Forces. He knows he couldn't be proved the father. What's he got to be afraid of? You tell me.'

'Not unless there's something we don't know.'

'There's plenty of that, lad. In a village like this one every family and every member of every family has got something to hide. And I'll tell you something else.

91

They'll gang up on us.' He lapsed into thought. 'No,' he resumed. 'We might have his garden up as a last resort but you realise what it would mean. Two things: he'd have had to bury her quickly and that night, and he's not a fit man. I really can't see him getting down in a hole and throwing out spadefuls of earth. It's either heart or blood pressure with him, I'll be bound; digging a grave would kill him. Come to think of it, I doubt if he'd have the strength to kill a powerful young girl. And another thing is: was it a quiet night? Look, I'll show you.'

He got out of the car and Quinney followed, noticing that Neill paid not the slightest attention to the fact that they were probably observed. They came round the side of the inn and looked across the piece of waste ground to Hades Flatt.

'See what I mean?' Neill nodded at the cottage. 'If any of them slept with their windows open, particularly the mother—Brenda—who wouldn't have slept much that night, he could never have dug a grave without someone hearing. There's less than fifty yards between his garden and that cottage. Why, she could have seen him if she'd leaned out of the window! Go back to the sub-station.'

'Renishaw?'

'Yes.'

'I thought we were going to see the gentry.'

'I've changed my mind.'

Quinney said nothing.

'Look,' Neill said explosively. 'What have we got? A girl's disappeared, right? But she's a tart. They ask for it all the time. It could have been anyone, if it *was* anyone—and how'd he dispose of her, anyway? Most likely prospect is like Lynch says: a passing motorist, a bit drunk, a bit mad—or both, and she's somewhere

92

in a wood between here and Sheffield under a layer of autumn leaves. That's *most* likely. Another possibility is the barn and a local chap other than Lynch. So while we're here we'll go and look at it because otherwise we'll just be sent back to do it and like as not there's nothing there, so we'll get that cleared now. We'll go up the way she'd have gone and we'll take a dog.'

'Renishaw took his dog before.'

'And it found a lipstick. We'll see if it can find anything else. But I'm not tackling a rich woman who probably does know the chief constable and saying to her: I found this lipstick in the woods, mum, is it yours and what were you doing there when you happened to drop it?'

Quinney drew up outside the sub-station and got out, hiding a grin. The old man had cold feet. All the same, he hoped they'd find something at the barn, something that would keep them in Bardale. He wanted to meet this lady whom he admired already, who wore white suède and was, according to Renishaw, no better than she should be.

Neill had a bad time getting up the path. He was in town shoes, of course, and he was old and heavy. Quinney, wearing similar footgear, fared better; he was agile and accustomed to slime in caves and pot-holes. Neill had to concentrate on the going, leaving the others to watch the terrier but, apart from rabbit scents, the dog showed no interest in the woods.

The barn was dark, nearly all the windows blocked with straw and sacking against the draughts. They opened the big double doors to get some light and then the detectives saw that the ground floor was partitioned. The space they stood in took up half the area and it was deep in dried mud and dung.

93

'The other half is a shippon,' Renishaw told them. 'Above us there's an old hay loft running the length of the upper floor.'

Despite the barn's solid appearance from the outside, the interior wasn't in such good condition. At one time there had been a flight of wooden steps leading to the loft but these had collapsed and access to the upper floor could be made only by standing on the side of a stall in the shippon and muscling through a hole in the ceiling. Neill sent Quinney up but the sergeant reported that the place was bare except for some worm-eaten planking.

Suddenly a new voice demanded belligerently:

'What's tha doing in my barn, eh?'

'That's Padley, the farmer,' Renishaw said quietly, and performed introductions, stressing Neill's rank. This made no impression on Padley, a small aggressive man apparently more upset by their presence than the reason for it.

'Tha should have asked permission,' he told Neill. 'Ah've had enough this weekend what wi' open gates and beasts all down to road. Look at me 'ay!'

'What hay?'

'Yo' mun ask. Ah had a tidy bit in yon end till them left door open, tha knows. Beasts got in and trampled it all over.'

'Who left the door open?'

'Them as cooms up 'ere where they've no right.'

'Who?'

'Ah got summat else ta do wi' me time than bother wi' "who". 'Ooligans, that's who!'

'When was this?'

'Sat'day night. Young Sue Stanton got beasts back o' Sunday. An' 'er and doctor's lads on ponies! If one o' me beasts 'ad broke its leg, who'd 'a paid for it, eh?'

94

A new thought struck him. 'Suppose it was me *bull!*'
His voice broke.

'Was there much hay?' Neill asked.

'Enough.'

'Where?'

'In yon end, Ah tell't 'ee.'

The detectives walked over and studied the spot indicated. There were a few more stalks in this corner but the bullocks had reduced it to the same bare mess as the rest of the barn.

'You'd have to go through that with a tooth comb,' Quinney said.

'What would you be looking for?' Neill asked him coldly.

Quinney didn't reply because he didn't want to be snubbed in front of the others but he considered the answer. Ear-rings? Fag ends? But those wouldn't be remarkable. They weren't after evidence of courting couples, but evidence of foul play—like blood. And that the dog would have found soon enough. He looked round. Padley and Renishaw were watching them.

'Where's your dog?'

'Me dog?' Renishaw started. 'Oh, he's around.'

But he wasn't. Renishaw went outside, calling. Quinney followed. The constable started round the barn and when he reached the second corner the terrier came to meet him. The animal looked shifty and gave his master a wide berth.

'Where you come from?' Renishaw asked, walking on. Now they were on the north side of Jagger's, facing Foodale. One entered the barn on this side by way of a set of half-doors which led to the shippon. These were closed. Outside them a small cobbled ramp sloped to the level of the yard. Renishaw stopped a few feet from the ramp and the dog, which had followed warily, halted some distance away.

'So what you find, lad?' Renishaw asked pleasantly.

The terrier wagged his tail.

'You'm a good lad,' Renishaw said with feeling. 'Seek then, seek on!'

The dog was torn between obedience and an obvious dislike of the order. It wriggled and whined, creeping nearer. Neill came round the corner, followed by Padley.

'Stay there, sir,' Renishaw said quietly. 'The dog's on to something.'

They watched it squirming on its belly. Renishaw kept up a string of blandishments. Quinney, who'd owned dogs himself, felt a thrill, a smell of horror....

'So!' Renishaw breathed softly.

The dog snuffed the cobbles once, started to retreat, only to be recalled. With mounting confidence it smelt the stones, tail wagging hysterically. It started to give small stifled barks. The whole performance had something of the obscene about it.

Neill approached and the dog backed off, ignored. The police looked at the cobbles thoughtfully.

'Which door do they use at night?' Neill asked Padley.

'This 'n.'

They transferred their attention to the half-doors which were shabby, with all the paint worn away so that they were now a dull shade of grey: very old, long-seasoned wood with cracks between the planks, a stain or two, and bright red hairs, short and coarse, on the jamb.

'Devon or Shorthorn,' Quinney said absently.

'Shorthorn,' Padley said.

'And that one?' Neill asked, and Quinney, looking to see the direction of his glance, saw the inspector's lip

96

lift in his mirthless grin. His eyes were no longer apathetic.

It was a long hair, about eight inches long, finer than that of a bullock, and very dark, black perhaps. It was caught in a splinter and the wood around it was smeared dark brown.

Chapter 7

'THIS IS MOST intriguing,' Ruth said. 'I write crime stories.'

She motioned Neill to sit down and he did so with his back to the view and the light. She ensconsed herself on the sofa and studied him with interest, apparently indifferent to the fact that this was reciprocal.

She wasn't wearing the cream suit but old cord trousers and an Aran pullover with an emerald shirt. Her hair was loose, she wore no make-up and she looked about thirty.

Remembering her manners, she offered him a drink, but he declined. She frowned and asked if he would like tea. This he accepted and she went out, to return shortly and settle herself again. She looked at him expectantly.

Neill showed no sign of dislike for the interview but waded straight in now that he had a definite idea of what the job was all about:

'I hear from the farmer, Padley, that your daughter was riding near Jagger's Barn yesterday.'

Ruth hesitated, giving the inspector time to wonder if she was naturally cautious. She didn't look it.

'Yes,' she said slowly.

'Apparently the children found all the gates and barn doors open, and the cattle out.'

His interest astonished her.

'Why on earth are you concerning yourself with straying bullocks?'

'Because,' Neill said deliberately, 'Jagger's Barn is where Judy Scroop met her friends.'

'Oh.' She paused. 'You've come to investigate that. You suspect foul play. I'm not surprised. But—the barn! And Saturday night! You don't think that when the children were up there Sunday that— Oh, my God, is she up there—in the barn?'

She stared out of the window and across the ravine.

'That's it,' she said. 'There's someone in the yard. Is that right?'

'She isn't in the barn.'

'But you've found her.'

'No.'

'Then what's that person doing in the yard? Who is he?'

'It's your constable, Renishaw, and he's making sure nothing is tampered with.'

'What have you found?'

He reached in his pocket and produced the Dior lipstick in a transparent plastic bag. He passed it to her without removing the covering.

'Have you seen this before?'

She held it by the plastic and turned it in order to see the maker's name and shade.

'It's mine.'

'You're sure?'

She looked again, suspecting a trap.

'No, I'm not sure. I had one, the same make, the same shade.'

'What happened to it?'

'I lost it. Where did you find this?'

'In the woods below Jagger's Barn.'

99

Ruth laughed in disbelief: 'That's impossible.' She corrected herself. 'In that case, it's not mine.' She stopped and thought, while he watched her. 'It's possible that I gave it to Judy,' she said. 'I give her things when I get tired of them.'

'She worked for you?'

'On and off. The women in the Street are a kind of labour pool. We employ them all, according to who is free—or fit. The wife of the quarry foreman is helping me at the moment because her daughter-in-law is expecting a baby.'

'Was Judy working for you Saturday?'

'No, for Miss Jebb, who lives next door.'

'When did she last work for you?'

'You'd have to ask my husband; I've been away for three months. Marilyn—that's my present help's daughter-in-law, was here when I came back. She's the better worker; I suspect my husband laid Judy off for a while. She was willing but slapdash.'

'Honest?'

'Superlatively.'

'You're very certain.'

'They all are, even Judy who wasn't very intelligent. *Isn't*, I mean. You don't *know* that something's happened to her, do you?'

He showed the canine tooth.

'Did she pilfer?'

'Most definitely not. I've told you.'

She was not calm enough to reflect that such questions would not have been put to a person in her position without good reason.

'Or pick up some little thing she took a fancy to?'

'That's still a euphemism for stealing. Judy doesn't steal.' She stopped and her eyes narrowed.

'Yes?' Neill asked smoothly.

100

'There's no need to steal,' she went on. 'I give her most of my clothes.'

'And cosmetics?'

'And cosmetics. They go with the clothes. When I buy new outfits, I buy new shades of cosmetics. They're complementary.'

'Indeed,' Neill said. 'I didn't know that.'

'And I give her odd things I've grown tired of: trinkets, perfume, little bits and pieces. I'm a very extravagant woman....'

She stopped again; they both knew she was being garrulous. Her eyes went to the window.

'Don't inspectors normally have sergeants with them?'

'Yes; he's getting someone to take the barn door to the laboratory.'

She stared at him.

'There's a long black hair on it and some brown stains.'

'On the *door*! You mean an old door, lying on the ground?'

'No, in place.'

There were steps in the passage and Annie Hibbert came in, carrying a tray set for one. She was wearing a maroon dress and white apron. Ruth made room on a table beside Neill and lit a lamp behind him. He raised his eyebrows at her and she was forced to introduce Annie.

'Do you know Judy Scroop, Annie?' he asked.

The woman twisted her fingers nervously and stared at him.

'We all know her,' she said.

'When did you see her last?'

She looked at Ruth helplessly.

'Sit down, Annie,' the younger woman told her. 'There's nothing to worry about.'

'I'm all right, mum. I can't say rightly. I suppose I saw her Saturday some time.'

'What time?'

'I can't say. Expect I see her every day. You see everybody some time, in a village. Did I see her that day?' Annie addressed her employer who smiled in sympathy.

'It really is difficult,' Ruth said to Neill. 'Particularly when one reaches middle-age—' her wry smile made it plain that she included herself in that category. '—One forgets whether things happened yesterday or the day before. *I* remember seeing Judy Saturday morning because it was my first day at home and she was wearing an old coat of mine and I thought how good she looked.' Ruth's hand went to her mouth, then she continued colourlessly: 'Annie's usually at the back of her house and she wouldn't see Judy pass up the Street.'

'How do you get on with her?' Neill asked the woman.

'I pass the time of day with Brenda Scroop and her girl.' The thin mouth shut tight like a clam.

'Nothing more than that?'

'We have nothing in common, sir.'

It was a rebuke but Neill persisted.

'Do you know where she meets her friends?'

Annie's head jerked and she stared out of the window towards the darkening terrace. They couldn't see her eyes.

'Yes,' she said.

'Who is her present boy friend?'

'I don't gossip.'

'I'll be the judge of whether it's gossip.' His tone was hard and the two women stiffened, their attention sharpening.

'Well?'

'She has several.'

'What are their names?'

'Bill Lynch,' Annie said quietly.

'And the others?'

'That's all I know.'

He nodded, dismissing her.

'That's it, thank you.'

Annie moved to the window and drew the curtains. 'You knew about Bill Lynch already,' Ruth stated when the woman had gone.

At this point Ned entered the sitting room. He looked inquisitive and wary. As Ruth was making the introductions, the door bell rang and Quinney was shown in. Annie was sent away for another cup and additional scones, Ruth switched on more lamps, Ned threw a log on the fire and dusted his hands, glancing doubtfully at the drinks on the sideboard.

Neill said nothing but concentrated on his tea. Quinney, trying to emulate him, felt hot and clumsy. Ruth, having seen that they had all they wanted, threw a glance at her husband and excused herself, saying that she must lend a hand with the dinner.

When she'd gone, Neill looked round the room, very much at his ease.

'We don't often find ourselves in such comfortable surroundings,' he said pleasantly. 'We see a lot of hotels: garish places, very impersonal. This is homely.' His hooded eyes rested casually on a Buhl writing desk. 'It's a pity to be working.' His gaze returned to Ned. 'It's a point,' he said conversationally: 'Is a sordid crime solved more easily in a sordid atmosphere or a tasteful one? Of course, you get sordid crimes in the most beautiful surroundings. Look at the murders that take place in bluebell woods, under hedgerows in spring.'

He stopped and Ned came in as if cued:

'Love nests,' he said. 'Pretty furnishings, tucked away down country lanes.'

'Exactly.'

'I've done a bit of crime reporting. Sometimes it's poignant, but it's always incongruous. A dead body is too unnatural.'

'That's only the first reaction,' Neill said. 'If you know the movements of the victim prior to her death, you lose the incongruity—eventually. Right now we're puzzled. Why did Judy Scroop go to meet her lover in Jagger's Barn on Saturday night? Dirty and uncomfortable was how it struck us, wouldn't you say, sergeant?'

Quinney nodded.

Ned didn't respond.

'Curious,' the inspector went on. 'Of course, we don't *know* anything, not till we get a laboratory report on the door.'

'What door?'

'Brown stains and a long black hair.'

'On the door,' Ned repeated. 'What does it mean?'

'As I said, we don't know, but if the blood's from the head, as the hair leads us to suppose, then it's probably the old blunt instrument: spanner, hammer, iron bar. He lay in wait for her as she arrived.'

'The hair could be from a bullock's tail.'

'Possibly.'

'And what makes you think it's human blood?'

'We don't, but it can be matched.'

'With what? How do you know her blood group?'

'The local maternity hospital will have it.'

'Did you find signs of this chap who lay in wait?'

'No. Any idea who he might be?'

Ned pondered.

'No,' he said at length as if contradicting himself. 'Lynch wouldn't leave the Woman. No need to. There wasn't anyone else. Must have been a stranger.'

'No one beside Lynch?' Neill said in disbelief.

'No one that I know of.'

'You knew her quite well then?'

'Everyone knew Judy.'

'She was working for you when your wife was abroad. Why did she leave?'

Ned looked uncomfortable.

'Had to give her the push,' he said.

'Why?'

'No good. Couldn't even do plain cooking. Couldn't clean. She was a bad influence. There's our daughter, you see.'

'Mrs Stanton didn't seem to mind Judy working here.'

'She behaved herself while my wife was home. Judy was no match for her.'

'Your wife kept her in order?'

'Oh yes. Judy had a great respect for her.'

'And you?'

'What's that?'

'I understand that Mrs Stanton is a very successful author and quite wealthy.'

'That is so.'

'And you run the house.'

'My wife does a lot of travelling and when she's home I like to save her the domestic chores.'

'So in fact, the traditional roles are reversed: your wife is the bread-winner, and you are the housewife—I beg your pardon—I should have said a kind of house-keeper?' Neill ended on an interrogatory note, raising his eyebrows.

Ned's face sagged and his eyes looked lifeless.

'Yes,' he said with quiet bitterness. 'You can call it that.'

'Stop at the bottom of the drive,' Neill said. 'Out of sight of the house.'

105

Quinney pulled the car in under a huge rhododendron. The inspector lit a cigarette and inhaled thankfully.

'These non-smoking households!' he grumbled.

'Somebody had told him,' Quinney remarked. 'He wasn't surprised about the barn, and not surprised enough about the door.'

Neill hazarded a guess:

'Someone telephoned while we were talking to his wife. The door was closed part of the time. Half the village will know by now. Padley saw the stains on the door, remember.'

'I didn't hear a telephone, did you?'

'It's one of those new warblers. Under a window in the passage outside the lounge. You missed it. He knew but his wife didn't. Well, he certainly knew, but was she shamming? The blood and hair on the door seemed to come as a shock to her. It's much too near home, of course. These three houses must be closer to that barn than the village street: more accessible to it, anyway; you could get a car up from here.'

'No,' Quinney said. 'The ruts are too deep. You'd take the sump off a car.'

He wound down the window; the smoke was getting in his eyes.

'You crowded Stanton hard,' he said.

'I was being damned impertinent,' Neill corrected, 'but he took it, every word. Now wouldn't you think a chap of that class would come back with a cold statement that the family's financial arrangements and their domestic set-up was nothing to do with Judy Scroop in Jagger's Barn, in fact, that it was no business of ours? Look at Lynch: he blustered like mad, but this one took it like a lamb—except at the very last. Deep waters, there. I'd like to know why Judy Scroop left his employment.'

'Wonder what his alibi will be for Saturday night?'
Neill gave a bark of amusement.

'How much do you bet every husband in this place was tucked up in bed on Saturday night from ten till dawn on Sunday?'

A vehicle passed the end of the drive, going uphill.

'One of our Land Rovers,' Neill mused. 'How were they getting on with those cobbles when you left?'

'They'll be a while yet.'

'Right, we'll go and have a word with the doctor.'

Lights blazed from Yaffles but were lost sight of as the drive curved and approached the house by way of a cobbled yard. At right angles to the main building a dimmer light showed amazingly clean windows and through a half-door that was ajar they heard young voices.

'See if you can find out why those gates were open Sunday morning,' Neill whispered.

'We haven't got the parents' permission—'

'So what? You're the chauffeur, just waiting for me. You can get into conversation can't you? There's not much of an age gap.'

He moved away. Quinney hesitated for a moment then walked towards the stables.

'... quite impossible,' came a boy's voice. '*Ascaris lumbricoides* in its larval form arrives in the stomach from the bronchi, *not* by ingestion.'

'But the p.m. definitely showed earthworms in her intestines.' This was a girl who sounded well-meaning but confused.

'The morphology is entirely different,' put in a younger boy.

Quinney coughed unhappily and put his head round the half-door.

'Good evening,' he said. 'I'm a chauffeur. Can I wait in the warm?'

A number of ponies' rumps were towards him and a boy of about thirteen was combing a tail. Heads lifted with a rattle of wood on wood and he seemed surrounded by eyes. Among the backs he saw a girl with long red hair and an older boy.

'Come in and shut the door,' the boy said. 'Who are you driving?'

'A detective-inspector.'

'What?' The smaller boy turned big eyes on him. 'What's it about?'

'Missing persons.'

'Olive Lynch,' the girl said. 'She's in—'

She stopped and the small boy giggled.

'She's where?'

'Nothing. We make jokes about it. Sick jokes. We're at that age.' She regarded him solemnly. She was a charmer and he was uncomfortably aware of how mature they could be at this age.

'You're not really a chauffeur,' the older boy said. 'An inspector doesn't rank one.'

'Some of them do.'

The girl leaned on her pony's back and surveyed him.

'What's happening at Jagger's?' she asked.

'They're poking around. It's just a gesture. They won't find anything because there were cattle inside at the weekend—'

'Don't we know it!' The smaller boy interrupted him. 'I reckon we had more to do with those bullocks than old Padley. I've still got the bruises to prove it. One jumped off the top of Magg's Tor!'

'That's a slight exaggeration,' the girl said. 'It jumped

108

about ten feet off the side and it got up and walked away.'

'Well, I fell after it.'

'That was your clumsiness,' his brother said grandly. 'And nothing to swank about.'

'Do you normally graze your cattle on cliffs in this part of the world?' Quinney asked innocently, sending the smaller boy into paroxysms.

'Don't mind him,' the other said. 'No. All the gates were open. The bullocks should be in the Outlands, that's the field where Jagger's Barn is, but they'd gone through the yard and in the barn, and down the track towards the road as well.'

'What time was this?'

'When we got there? After breakfast. What time was it, Sue?'

'I don't know.' The girl sounded sullen.

'Nine-thirty,' the smaller boy said promptly.

'Was anyone else about at that time in the morning?'

'If anyone was, they were in the barn, but we wouldn't notice because we were watching the going. The ponies were all fresh and there are rabbit holes on the Outlands. They could break their legs,' he explained, in case Quinney didn't know. 'That's why we didn't notice that the gates were open.'

'But I thought you said—'

'I saw them,' the smaller one interrupted. 'But I thought Padley was in the barn. You would, wouldn't you, with the half-doors open as well?'

'Why are you so interested?' the girl asked aggressively, but the smaller boy was rattling on:

'And it wasn't till we came back hours later that it really penetrated and I thought old Padley must still be in the barn and had had an accident or something. The loft floor's all wormy. So we went in and no one was there, and then we heard the cattle down in the woods. The little gate was open too.'

'Were all the barn doors open?' Quinney asked.

'Not the double doors; just the half-doors on the north side.'

'Why *are* you so interested?' The older boy echoed the girl.

Quinney frowned.

'I don't know. The boss thinks it's funny. At one time he seemed to have the idea that the barn could have been used for stolen goods, somewhere to unload a hijacked lorry for instance. After all, it's not far from the motorway—'

'Not a hope,' said the smaller boy. 'There were no tracks; we looked specially.'

'What made you think of a vehicle at all?' Quinney asked.

'Because if you're going through a gate on foot, you close it or, if you're lazy, you leave it to swing. This one had been propped open.'

'Propped?'

'Yes, with an old pitch fork. It used to be in the loft.'

'It had occurred to me,' Neill said with satisfaction as they descended Foodale. 'The bullocks were let in deliberately, to cover tracks and blood. It's too much of a coincidence otherwise.'

'It must be a countryman,' Quinney said. 'More than that, it's a local. He knew about the pitch fork. But he reckoned without the laboratory. If she was killed there, we'll find traces under those cobbles. Blood seeps deep.'

'Really?'

Quinney crashed his gears.

Chapter 8

BY TEN O'CLOCK the cobbles had been taken up and a second Land Rover left for the laboratory. The first one had taken the barn door. Uniformed police had been drafted in and they had started to search the woods, with more hindrance than help from floodlights mounted on top of the cliffs in a line from Magg's Tor. After one man had fallen over a small outcrop and crippled himself by pulling a muscle, Neill postponed further search until first light, but the floods stayed mounted, beaming down through a tracery of trees. Against them the pinnacles and towers looked like the fairy background to a Renaissance painting rather than the heart of modern England.

'If she's there,' Neill remarked with ghoulish satisfaction, 'no one's going to try moving her tonight.'

They were standing on the upper bridge, looking down the dale. The nearer cliffs were silhouetted against the glare, and there were strange shadows below in the Street. Suddenly they were aware of a dim glow on their right and a door slammed. Figures crossed the road. They moved forward.

'Good evening,' Quinney said.

''Evening.' In the light of a torch Joe Hibbert's face looked lined and old.

'Mr Hibbert?'

'That's right.'

'Night shift?'

'Yes. Ten to six.'

'And who are you?' Neill asked the other.

'Michael Hibbert. He's my dad.'

'Are you on the night shift too?'

'Ay.'

'So you'll both be off at six.'

'That's right,' Joe said.

'We won't keep you.'

The police went back to the bridge.

'All one big happy family,' Quinney said facetiously.

Neill grunted and lit a cigarette.

'Did you notice,' Quinney went on, 'that they both came out of the same house?'

There was no reply. An engine started and lights came on. A Land Rover eased out of the garage and turned down the Street.

'Lazy,' Quinney said with disapproval. 'They ought to walk; it's no distance.'

Still Neill said nothing. The end of his cigarette glowed. Quinney would have liked to sit on the parapet and contemplate the dark water below but he reckoned that if the old man was so deep in thought, he should at least appear to be thinking himself. So he remained upright, staring idly at the blueish light through the trees and wondering if the Wild Boar could be induced to serve ham and eggs after closing time.

Neill came out of his reverie.

'Fastidious, would you say?'

Quinney blinked.

'Who?'

'Ruth Stanton.'

'Oh, definitely.'

The little red glow turned towards him. Now there

would be some cutting remark about sixth form enthusiasm. But Neill was following a train of thought.

'Would she give away a used lipstick even to the help?'

'She wouldn't and she didn't.'

'She tried to make us think she did though. And something else: perfume, she said she gave the girl, and trinkets—all little things that could be picked up easily and slipped in a pocket. If she thinks we're going to search the girl's room and knows we're going to find a hoard of her own stuff, she's explaining it away in advance. But we agree she wouldn't give away a used lipstick, so is the whole explanation a lie?'

'I don't get it,' Quinney said. 'If she's trying to make out it was Judy Scroop dropped the lipstick in the woods, why doesn't she admit the girl nicked it, that she's in the habit of nicking things?'

'Because she wasn't. That can be proved by her other employers. If she pilfered from one, she'd pilfer from them all.'

'So Ruth Stanton dropped the lipstick.'

'Oh no. She recognised it. If she'd dropped it, she'd have known where. Even rich women don't lose good stuff like this without at least some idea of where and when. If she's up to anything dishonest, from deceiving her husband to murder, she'd have worked out almost immediately where she dropped that lipstick, and she'd have a story ready.'

Quinney blinked in the dark, wondering how the old man had picked up this knowledge of the behaviour of guilty wives.

'I'm like Renishaw,' he said. 'I don't believe Ruth Stanton would meet a man in that barn. It was in a disgusting state.'

'Not good enough for you?' Neill asked nastily. 'I

don't believe she dropped it, or knows anything about it since it was nicked—probably by the husband.'

'Stanton?.'

'It figures. He's got no money. Men like to give girls presents, particularly middle-aged men and young girls. What's easier than to pick up the odd thing of his wife's and give it to the girl friend? *She* realised that. She's nobody's fool, that woman, and for all I don't hold with these fancy crime books, people who write them seem to know a bit about human nature—quite a bit about how we operate too,' he added morosely.

'What did you make of the Edens?' Quinney asked.

'Nothing special about the wife,' Neill told him. 'Plain, tweeds and silk blouse, you know the sort; dumpy but a lady. Lot of money there: quiet, warm air *and* a log fire, like the Stantons', thick carpets, huge radiogram, classy place; a nice lot of drinks on the side, colour television.'

You had a drink too, you selfish old bloodhound, Quinney thought. He could smell the Scotch.

'It was just a social call,' came from the darkness, as if Neill were clairvoyant. 'He's different.'

'The doctor?'

'If Renishaw hadn't briefed us, I'd have wondered. Stares at you very hard, waits before he speaks. A very careful bird, was my impression.'

'Local man?'

'Not from this dale, but born only ten miles off.'

'Good enough. Is he careful because he's a killer, or is he protecting someone—like a priest?'

'You're really on the ball tonight,' Neill said. 'We haven't got a body yet.'

'Men have been convicted without a body.'

'Not many, lad. I know we've got some blood and a hair, and we've got her hair brush. It was a good idea of yours, by the way, putting a man in the Woman. I wouldn't care to be in Bill Lynch's shoes when Brenda Scroop realises why we wanted that brush. I've little doubt it's her daughter's hair on the door—but that's not a body. We've got to find her.'

'We'll do that. We'll have the dogs tomorrow.' Quinney spoke with assurance.

'I hope so. I expect so. But how many people have disappeared in the past few years, most of them probably murdered, some of them certainly, and no body's shown up?'

'We got here within two days—less. We've got a head start. And no one's searched the woods. Renishaw just went up the path to the barn—or down it.'

'What's the depth of soil under these trees?'

'You're right. It's mainly scree. If there's any soil, it's just a skin.'

Quinney turned to look upstream. Nothing showed in the dark except points of reflected light on the wall bounding Bardale Bank but he remembered the lie of the land.

'There's a bit of meadow land here, below the road, and there's the Outlands, and of course there's people's gardens.'

'Whose gardens?'

There was a long pause. The floods glared implacably from the cliffs but the dale was curiously quiet. No cars passed and they could hear no sound of television or conversation from behind the closed doors in the Street. A leaf fluttered here and there, pale smoke rose from dark chimneys, the odd aerial gleamed in the light. Up in Foodale there was a sudden ghastly screech.

'*What the hell!*'

'Fox,' Quinney said, grinning.

'We'll get back,' Neill said after a long moment which

he must have needed to regain control: 'I feel I'm being listened to here.'

The proprietor of the Wild Boar was a retired policeman. Quinney had booked accommodation earlier in the evening, and now they were told to make themselves comfortable while a late supper was cooked. The man brought them beer and went out, closing the door carefully.

They sat opposite each other and took deep draughts of bitter, then Neill leaned back and regarded his sergeant.

'Whose gardens?' he repeated.

Quinney had the impression the old man was asking the question of himself as well.

'Do we include Bull Low?'

'No, we start with the Street and we include Foodale. This is a *very* local man. He knew about those bullocks *and* the pitch fork, remember. Make a list. Start with Foodale.'

'Ned Stanton.'

'Motive?'

'She was making trouble. Wanted marriage or money or both. He hit her—'

'What with?'

'Something lying in the barn; there's always some old iron lying about a barn.'

'But not handy, and in the dark, don't forget that. You might think he'd hit her with his fist, or strangle her, but you wouldn't expect him to have an iron bar in his hand when they started to quarrel.'

'He was lying in wait for her.'

'More like it, lad, more like it. Not a sudden quarrel then, is it? Never mind. How did he get away from home without anyone noticing after ten on Saturday night, or was he out all the time, and if so, where? We'll want to know Mr Stanton's movements all evening, particularly after ten, and his real relations with the help. I don't think they were that of employer and employee somehow.

'Next down Foodale comes the doctor. Motive?, Hm. I suppose we can assume, for the time being anyway, that in the case of Judy Scroop and married men, the motive was roughly similar: removing a threat to their security—at least till we unearth something to the contrary. It follows we have to establish the relationship of every man in the village with her. We might do better to consider opportunity. Where was the doctor after ten on Saturday?'

Quinney wrote in his notebook.

'We'll leave out the Eden boys,' Neill went on. 'There have been killers that young—but we'll put them on one side for the moment. And that brings us to Joe Hibbert. At ten he went on shift.'

'You sure?' Quinney asked, pen poised.

'Ah. Change of shift?'

'Very likely. Sunday was probably the start of the night shift. He could have been on from six a.m. till two p.m., or two till ten on Saturday.'

'Check it. I wonder what kind of a man Joe Hibbert is. Taciturn and powerful was the impression I got in the darkness. We'll spend some time on the Street tomorrow. There's the son too. Burglary, now going straight, according to Renishaw. Small-time villains aren't big-time criminals but they're often unstable characters. Yes, we're interested in Michael Hibbert and his movements on Saturday evening. Same shift as his father last week, I suppose, since they're going to work together this week.'

'That could be significant.'

'How's that?'

'Almost as if they wanted to keep an eye on him.'

'Could be. You notice all these fellows are married, with devoted wives.'

'Who says they're devoted?'

There was a knock on the door and the ex-policeman and his wife came in with a loaded tray and a large earthenware jug of beer. When they'd gone and the detectives had taken the edge off their appetites, Neill asked:

'Do you know who lives in the other houses in the Street?'

'There's only two other families. I know who they are, but not where they come in sequence.'

'No matter for the moment.' Neill showed his long tooth. 'Not until we get down to taking up paving stones in back yards. Who are they?'

'Padley.'

'Oh yes.'

'Then there's an old chap who's an invalid and confined to a wheel chair, and an empty house with the doctor's surgery on the ground floor—and that's it, except for the Woman.'

'So with Bill Lynch,' Neill counted on his fingers. 'Leave out the invalid; Padley, the Hibberts, Eden and Stanton, we've got six.'

'That's the long list. We can knock off Lynch—you reckon.'

Neill chewed a piece of bread and stared grimly at a black and brown oil of a spaniel.

'Padley, the two Hibberts, Stanton and John Eden,' he intoned. 'Suppose, just for a moment, he was lying in wait at Jagger's, struck at her as she came up the cobbles—then it was premeditated and not a spontaneous outburst of violence. Premeditation means careful calculation. Who would you say of those five has got the most to lose?'

Quinney's answer was prompt:

'Moneywise: Ned Stanton.'

'And prestige, local standing?'

'I haven't see him. What about the doctor?'

'He's got no money either; it's all his wife's, according to Renishaw.'

'Stanton didn't impress me as a man who cared about money. How did you feel about Eden?'

'They don't care when they've got it. They forget where it comes from until there's a threat to their security, then they change into wolves.'

'You must have met it before.' The sarcasm was lost on Neill. 'Another thing is that only the two up Foodale have got gardens, leaving out Lynch. As you said, it's back yards and paving stones in the Street—unless, my God!'

'What?'

'Styx Hole!'

'That strikes a chord.'

'It would do more than that if you'd been here longer. It's opposite the Hibberts' place. I never thought about it while we were on the bridge. We were standing right across from the entrance—one of the entrances.'

'Deep, is it?'

'The ordinary route is three thousand feet long.'

'*Deep?*'

'No, it doesn't go down—well, only forty feet or so to start. Then it's more or less horizontal but there are a few pitches: that's up or down. There's water too. But there's more than one route; it's a maze. Some of it hasn't been explored.'

'You've been down there though.'

'I'd better go back and get my gear tomorrow.'

'Send for it. I need you here. Can we get some more men who'd know what they're doing down there?'

'About three, if you can get them off.'

'I'll get them,' Neill said with certainty. 'But I'll have those woods and gardens done first. Meanwhile you and me'll concentrate on the Street.'

Chapter 9

MARILYN TOOK A long time answering the door. Frail,
angry and obviously pregnant, she would be a daunting
figure to most men, and was to Quinney. Only Neill,
expecting it, saw the fear behind the mask, and noticed
the knuckles white on the door jamb.

'No,' she said tensely, in answer to his query. 'He's
sleeping; you'll have to come back.'

'Not this time,' Neill told her. 'Be a good girl and
tell him we're here.'

'He's working nights. He's worn out. He's in the
house; he won't run away.'

Neill looked past her, up the dark stairs to where a
shadow moved against daylight at the top. Michael Hibbert came down in his socks and with his shirt unbut-
toned. He grinned at them impudently and gestured
towards the back of the house.

'Come on in.' He put a hand on his wife's shoulder.
'Get us a cuppa, lass. We won't offer them the Scotch;
they're working.'

The kitchen was almost painfully neat with a black-
leaded range and a kettle boiling on the trivet. A cheap
new sideboard shone with wax, the plastic-topped table
was clean and bare, and a blue budgerigar pecked at
a tiny mirror in a white cage.

Michael Hibbert showed Neill to an easy chair and

took its twin for himself, leaving Quinney to sit at the table.

Joe Hibbert's son had neither his father's appearance of strength nor his mother's fine eyes. His features were unremarkable but his expression was sly. He studied every utterance to see how it might affect him but this examination was so adept that it proclaimed an habitual reaction rather than the fear of the police exhibited by almost everyone confronted by a detective investigating a murder.

Marilyn didn't go away. She made the tea while Neill told them factually and superfluously that the police were investigating the disappearance of Judy Scroop. The police had no doubt that by now everyone in Bardale knew that the dogs had arrived some time ago and had started to search the woods below the cliffs.

Young Hibbert gave them no help but watched Neill's face with an interest in which, Quinney felt, observing him from the side, there was a trace of amusement. But he noticed that when Marilyn poured the tea her hands were unsteady.

'So why come to me?' Hibbert asked at length.

'Because,' Neill said comfortably, 'we're interested in all the men who knew her.'

Hibbert said nothing.

'How well did you know her?' the inspector asked.

Quinney watched the girl and saw her chin lift in the slightest gesture of defiance—or defence. Her husband glanced at her too, and shrugged.

'All the chaps had known her, some time,' he said.

'By "known" you mean they were intimate with her?'

'Yeah; if that's what you call it.'

'Were you still intimate with her?'

'No.'

It was stated coolly, as a fact, with no indignation.

Neill looked at Marilyn.

'I'd have known if he was,' she said, but she couldn't achieve the same lack of expression as her husband. That didn't have to mean she lied; her anxiety might be due merely to the fact that wives of even petty criminals have more to worry about than wives of law-abiding men.

'Where would you be on Saturday night?' Neill asked in what for him was a friendly tone.

Marilyn stiffened and seemed to hold her breath.

'I was in Sheffield,' Hibbert said.

'Where?' Neill pressed.

'The Blue Lagoon.'

Quinney's biro stopped suddenly. He remembered the check on the three Bull Low lads who had been in the Quiet Woman on Saturday night. The Blue Lagoon was the club they'd visited in Sheffield, but when they reached it there was a fourth member in their party. The proprietor remembered them. It had been a slack night.

'Are you a member?' Neill asked.

'I joined on Saturday.'

So there'd be a record—if the place kept books. So why hadn't the proprietor named him? Because, Quinney thought wryly, answering his own thought, he wasn't asked. Four lads from Bardale, he'd said, and they'd assumed Hughie Blount and company had picked up a pal on the way. And so they had—or had they?

'What time did you leave here?' Neill asked.

'Here? This house?'

'Why not?'

'I left the house at two o'clock, after me dinner.'

'Where did you go then?'

'To work.'

'Two to ten shift?'

123

'That's right.'

'What time did you leave the quarry?'

'At ten.' Hibbert evinced surprise.

Marilyn hadn't relaxed and she didn't touch her tea. She was very white.

'Tell us what you did after ten.'

The lad glanced at Quinney who waited to take it down.

'I walked down the road,' he began slowly, noticed Quinney used shorthand, raised his eyebrows in mock surprise and speeded up: 'Me mates picked me up, as arranged, at road-end. That would be about five past ten. Twenty-two five,' he translated for Quinney in an aside. The sergeant felt a muscle tighten in his cheek. He stared at Hibbert coldly, measuring him.

'Then we went to the Blue Lagoon,' the lad ended with deliberate lameness.

'Names of your mates?' Neill asked.

'Hughie Blount, Jake Newton, Tom Bagshawe.'

'You can give the addresses to Sergeant Quinney afterwards. How long were you at the club?'

'Very late. I don't know. Got home after two.'

He glanced at his wife.

'You came in at quarter past three,' she said tightly.

'I suppose the club was crowded,' Neill remarked.

Young Hibbert grinned.

'Not all that much. A fair number saw us, including the man who runs it, and when we weren't watching the turns, we talked to the barmaid. She had pink hair. Hughie called her Ingrid.'

'You must get filthy, working in a lime quarry,' Neill said idly.

'Like millers.' He was chirpy as a cricket.

'How'd they come to let you into a club like that?'

He stared at Neill in astonishment.

'I'd never go in me working gear! I left me clothes in the car.'

'How did you get hold of decent gear?'

The police were on a losing streak and they knew it. The questions were just form.

'I had me slacks and sweater on underneath, didn't I?'

'And Hughie Blount and his mates will bear you out on that.'

'Oh, yeah. They'll do that.'

'Why didn't you come home and change?'

'*She* wouldn't have liked it.'

He grinned at his wife. Neill addressed the girl.

'Is he in the habit of doing this kind of thing?' he asked gently.

'Yes.'

'What do you think of it?'

'I don't like it, but he'll stop when the baby's born. I can't go out now.'

Neill stood up.

'Give those addresses to the sergeant, and don't go away. I'll be needing you some time today.'

'What for?' Marilyn asked.

Young Hibbert glanced at her in amused contempt.

'Identification,' he told her. 'They have to try to prove I wasn't in Sheffield on Saturday night.'

'We won't,' Quinney said softly, standing on the pavement outside and listening to the noise made by the searchers. In places they could see movement through the trees.

Neill drew on his cigarette.

'Ay.' He was very dour. 'He's not clever but he's quite confident. He knows he's got nothing to worry about.'

'Why's *she* worried then?'

'Occupational hazard of a good girl married to a crook. We'll see what the father's got to say now, before they've had the chance to put their heads together.'

He moved a few steps and lifted the knocker on the elder Hibbert's door. Joe Hibbert opened it and looked at them calmly. Like his son, he was in his shirtsleeves.

'Perhaps we can have a word with you now,' Neill suggested.

'Come inside.'

He showed them to the parlour and switched on the light. There was no fire. He appeared not to notice the cold but sat down on a shiny chair with a curved back and a horsehair seat. The detectives took easy chairs on either side of the empty grate which contained a pleated fan of red crêpe paper. Neill stared at Hibbert in silence but the foreman waited calmly, giving no sign of uneasiness.

'We have reason to believe that Judy Scroop has been the victim of foul play,' Neill began.

'That's bad,' Hibbert said gravely.

'What were your relations with the girl?'

'Neighbourly.'

'What does that mean exactly?'

'I'd pass the time of day with her; sometimes have a bit of a chat. She liked to talk.'

Neill continued to stare at him, then looked out of the window. After a while his gaze, full of misery, returned to Hibbert who hadn't moved. Quinney remembered that he watched birds.

'Where were you at ten o'clock on Saturday evening?'

'Exactly at ten?'

'Yes.'

'Probably looking at a kiln in the quarry.'

Neill nodded to himself. He glanced at Quinney who was making notes.

'Suppose you give us your movements from six o'clock that evening,' he suggested.

Like his son Hibbert had been on the two to ten shift last week and he obliged them with details of his evening's work. Quinney wrote diligently. There was nothing else to do. The man's face and voice were expressionless, and there was certainly nothing of charm or distinction to distract one in the poky little room. A naturalist Hibbert might have been; he was no collector, and all his books must have been in the living room. The parlour was dark, cold and dull.

The last thing Hibbert had done before he came off shift was to attend to an electrical fault in a kiln. The electrician had been with him. He'd finished about ten-thirty.

'Then?' Neill asked.

'I came home.'

'In the Land Rover?'

'No. I'd walked to work.'

'Of course, it's only a step, isn't it? But I noticed you used the Land Rover last night.'

'It's quite a way up the incline to the quarry. Over a mile, all told. We were a bit late last night.'

'You always go to work with your son?'

'I give him a lift if we happen to leave at the same time.'

'And come home together?'

'Not always. We don't always leave at the same time. I'm not a clock watcher.'

'So what happened Saturday?'

Hibbert showed his first sign of uneasiness and Quinney felt the same twinge of excitement he'd known when the dog had sniffed the cobbles. He watched the man intently. The foreman appeared to be listening.

'Go on,' Neill urged.

He looked at them doubtfully.

'I don't want his mother to know.'

Neill nodded to Quinney who got up and shut the door, glancing outside as he did so. There was no one in the passage.

'The boy's done a stretch,' Hibbert said.

'We know all about that. What happened Saturday night?'

'He went to a club in Sheffield.'

Neill leaned back in his chair and the tension was turned off like a tap.

'And his mother wouldn't like it,' the inspector observed with heavy sarcasm.

'One of the lads he went with was one he ran around with before.'

Neill lit a cigarette, inhaled deeply and relaxed. He looked bored.

Quinney took up the questioning.

'What time did he come home from Sheffield?'

'About three in the morning.'

'You heard him?'

'No, his wife told me. That's how I know it all. She's worried too. She wants him to keep straight.'

'How did he get on with Judy Scroop?' Neill put in unexpectedly.

Hibbert shrugged.

'You'd need to ask him, but I can tell you: he's not interested in girls outside his wife.'

Neill's eyes rested on Quinney for a moment, then:

'What time did you get home from work on Saturday?' he asked.

'About a quarter to eleven.'

'Then what did you do?'

'I had my supper, read a book for a bit and went to bed.'

'Where was your wife?'

'She served my supper and had a bite with me and a cup of tea. Then she did something, can't remember, knitting probably, until it was time for bed.'

Neill leered at Hibbert.

'Tell us, what did you think of Judy Scroop?'

'In what way?'

'Her sexual exploits.'

'That was nothing to do with me.'

'It's a small village, this part of it; a hamlet, you might say.'

'Ay.'

'And the girl's goings-on affected no one in the Street?' Neill's tone held a kind of laboured amusement.

'It didn't concern us.'

'Never? How long had the Scroops lived here?'

'About fifteen years.'

'Was there a man, a husband of Brenda?'

'They came here alone, just the two of them.'

'And Judy always confined her attentions to men outside the Street?'

'She never bothered me.'

'And you can't speak for anyone else.'

Neill waited but Hibbert had taken it for a statement, not a question.

'All right.' The inspector stood up. 'You'll see more of us.'

'Why?' Hibbert asked.

Neill looked at him coolly.

'Judy Scroop was knocked on the head at Jagger's Barn,' he said.

Hibbert frowned.

'How do you know?'

'Blood and hair on the door.'

'It needn't have been her.'

'It was hers. They've been checked in the laboratory.'

'She might be alive.'

'I didn't say she was dead. But it's likely, isn't it?'

He'd thought to end it there but Hibbert was pondering.

'Animals can survive terrible wounds,' he said as if to himself.

'This is a human being,' Neill said frostily.

As the detectives left the Hibberts' cottage the searchers were approaching Joe's garage. Neill looked at them sourly. They both knew nothing had been found.

'Turn 'em round and send 'em back again,' Neill ordered. 'I'll be in the shop.'

The two halves of Mrs Padley's door were so narrow he had to squeeze in sideways. They had glass panels which were hung with True Love stories, a Do-it-yourself magazine, comics and a grubby *Brides* dated last May. A bell tinkled gaily as he opened the door. It was the kind of old-fashioned general shop which he thought no longer existed and whose only concession to the space age was a freezer stocked with peas and fish fingers and ice cream. Bunches of coloured canvas boots dangled from the ceiling, along with hearth brushes, tinny saucepans, strings of onions, a man's suit and sticks of an insect repellent which was supposed to have been taken off the market nine months ago.

Mrs Padley was a fat and comfortable lady who smiled at him broadly. It made a change. He asked for twenty Players.

'Have you found anything?' she asked, handing him the cigarettes.

'No. You'd know if we had.'

'Not 'less I was told,' she responded cheerfully. She wasn't dumb, but then none of them was.

Neill sighed.

'You must have seen more of Judy Scroop than most,' he suggested, without much hope.

'I saw more of her mother. Judy wasn't one for doing the shopping.'

'I see. It's curious,' he said with deceptive candour, 'how a girl like Judy who got around so much, seemed to keep so quiet about it.'

Mrs Padley chuckled richly.

'Well, it be no good you asking women, would it now? It were men she liked.'

'You're not telling me the ladies didn't know what was going on?'

' 'Course we knew. Turned a blind eye, didn't we?'

'Was it everybody?'

She gave it a moment's thought.

'Yes, everybody. Didn't mean nothing though, did it? Just a bit of fun like. No one was worried.'

'No one was worried?'

'Why should they be?'

'Where was your husband on Saturday evening, Mrs Padley?'

She shook like a jolly jelly.

'We watched telly till eleven or so, then us went to bed. I know 'bout the door, o' course, Padley told me, but it weren't no one in Bardale. Nor in Foodale neither.'

'In Bull Low?'

'Bull Low!' She screeched with amused contempt. 'Why'd anyone down there want to do her in? They got nothing to be afraid of. They'm all the same at Bull Low. They gets it from the telly.'

With which ambiguous statement he had to be content. Quinney was outside and they strolled on, past what they now knew to be John Eden's surgery. Next door, at the end house in the terrace, they stopped

131

opposite Henry Raven's open window.

It was uncertain how long he'd been waiting but he was expecting them. As soon as they came within sight he started to wheeze with glee. Neill stared at him with distaste but this seemed to enhance Henry's enjoyment of the situation.

'All tangled up,' he chortled. 'Dog this way round tree, man t'other—never seen anything to touch it in all me born days. Ho!'

Neill and Quinney, who had tried to ignore the antics of the handlers and their leashed Alsatians on the steep wooded scree, could find nothing to say.

Henry composed himself.

'Found her?' he asked, with the sublime confidence of one who knows he can't be apprehended. Neill turned his back.

'Shall we?' Quinney asked.

Henry regarded the sergeant thoughtfully.

'Maybe.'

'Not in the woods,' Quinney suggested.

'No, not in them woods.'

'Other woods?'

'Where?' Henry asked innocently.

'Or the Outlands.'

'Maybe.'

'You wouldn't know,' Neill put in rudely. 'She was buried at night.'

'Was she now?' Henry breathed in wonder.

Neill stalked on towards the Quiet Woman. Quinney winked at Henry and sat on the window sill.

'Light me a fag, lad,' Henry pleaded. 'There they are: on table. She'll only give me one when she comes, and she won't come special. She'm down Woman now.'

Quinney swung his legs over the sill and performed this small service.

'Hold it for me between puffs,' Henry commanded. 'Ah can't lift me hands, see. Stay where you're near.' He peered at the sergeant. 'You'm a well set up lad to be in police force. Ah seen you somewheres.'

'Here in Bardale. I come caving.'

'Ah, I seen you walking up Street then. You been down Styx?'

'Yes.'

'And you'll be going down again.'

'Yes.' It came slower this time.

'Give us a puff. There. Ah got two pleasures left: watching, and me fags.'

'How many cavers are there in Bardale?'

'Most on 'em and none on 'em.'

'Meaning?'

'Us all messed about down Styx as lads, when we got old enough to defy our mums *and* dads, but we none of us was proper cavers like them as comes here in them overalls and hats at weekend.'

'Anyone could have done it,' Quinney said absently, proffering the cigarette.

'Except me.'

'Nice to be in the clear. No one else is.'

'Shouldn't wonder if'n you're right,' Henry said judiciously.

Quinney found Neill in the pub. Behind the bar was a small grey woman who must be Lily Raven.

'I've been talking to your husband,' Quinney said pleasantly.

'He makes things up,' Lily told him.

'What did he say?' Neill asked.

'About what?'

'Any ideas where Judy Scroop's body is?'

'Oh, he thinks it's down Styx Hole,' Quinney said

133

casually, drinking, and looking past his tankard at Lily. She didn't say anything.

'Would you think that was likely, Mrs Raven?' Neill asked.

'Could be.'

She held a glass up to the light, passed it and placed it on a shelf. She took another out of the sink under the bar and started drying it.

'No one seems particularly interested in the girl,' Neill said coldly. 'She was young and happy and from all accounts did no harm to anyone.'

Lily said nothing.

'What did you think of her?' Neill raised his voice, goaded.

'Me? I didn't think nothing. Why should I? I got my husband to look after. I got no time to think about young girls. That's a silly question.'

They went outside and, standing on the green, staring at Magg's Tor, Neill said what he thought of them: quietly but viciously. Quinney listened with half an ear. The old man was right; they didn't want to know, but was it callousness or a deliberate wall of silence?

They went up to the Outlands again where a number of men were examining the ground, working outwards from the barn. Renishaw could be seen among them, distinguished by slower and more careful movements.

'I don't think she's here,' Neill said, watching them. 'It's too open. I've phoned H.Q. and asked them to bring the proprietor of the Blue Lagoon across,' he added. 'But Michael Hibbert was in that club; I'm sure of it. If we could only find the body ... and find out how it was done.... The chaps you asked for should be here this afternoon. You can go down Styx Hole then.'

The inspector left a message with Renishaw saying

he was to be informed immediately if anything was found, that he didn't know where he'd be and it was up to the messenger to find him, then, with Quinney, he moved across the field towards Foodale.

They didn't go directly to the gate but stopped above the ravine to study the houses opposite.

'Beautiful sites for all of them,' Neill remarked. 'I can't get away from the fact that Stanton has got a sight more to lose than anyone else. I think we'll have a go at Miss Jebb. It won't hurt Stanton to stew a bit longer. Might do us some good if he knows we're going to all the neighbours.'

They transferred their attention to Catcliff.

It was a tall Victorian house of red brick, roofed with slate but the worst of its ugliness concealed by shrubs and trees. There was a noise of undergrowth being hacked and they became aware of someone working in the garden above the lane. A slasher rose, catching the light, and fell. A moment later the sound reached them.

'Would that be her?' Neill asked unhappily.

'I expect so.' Quinney didn't relish the look of Catcliff either; he would have preferred to give the redoubtable Miss Jebb a miss and go straight to Heathens' Low. True, their principal objective there would be Ned Stanton but they'd probably see the wife as well. He wondered whether Neill was considering interviewing husband and wife separately but speculation was interrupted by the sight of a car which came up Foodale and turned in the drive of Heathens' Low. It was a red Triumph and they recognised it as that belonging to the local crime reporter: Tom Pierce from the *Daily Graphic*.

'That's going to make him uneasy,' Neill murmured.

'Who?'

'Stanton. An intelligent killer wouldn't relish a Press interview.'

'Unless he was an exhibitionist.'

'Did he strike you like that?'

'Not really. He didn't mind talking though, did he?'

'Perhaps he was laying a foundation.'

'For?'

'An alibi. If he's selective about who he talks to, it'll be interesting. For instance, if he's in the house and won't see Pierce, *I* shall be interested. We'll go to Miss Jebb now and hope the Press have gone by the time we get to the Stantons.'

Emily Jebb was so handy with the slasher that it was quite frightening to be below her, even though they had halted some yards away in the lane. It was the Labrador that was first aware of them, setting up a din that stopped the old lady dead. Her withered-apple face appeared above the brambles.

'Good morning,' she mouthed through the noise. 'Quiet, Guinea, quiet. Here!'

The dog went to her and sat, alert. She fondled its ears.

'Guard dog,' she said with a sweet smile.

Neill introduced himself and Quinney and indicated that they would like to talk to her. She acquiesced graciously and they were directed down the lane and up the drive to the side of the house where they were joined by the owner and conducted without excuse to the back door. The bitch sniffed Neill's trouser legs suspiciously.

'She won't bite,' Emily said, but her tone lacked conviction.

The dog was shut out and they were shown in to a large kitchen warmed by an old-fashioned coal stove. The table was of heavy white wood, far older than the house, although it was so cumbersome and heavy that either the kitchen must have been built round it, or it had come through the door in sections. It looked as if generations of farming Jebbs had sat down to eat from it.

There were three wicker chairs, on one of which the tortoiseshell queen nursed a litter of kittens.

Emily seated her guests and, ignoring the cats, took a hard kitchen chair for herself. Quinney realised, with a touch of amusement, that they were to be treated as tradesmen rather than the kind of visitor who warranted the superior atmosphere of a reception room. Accordingly, he got up and seated himself opposite Emily at the table. She glanced at him in reproof.

'The basket chair is more comfortable,' she chided.

'I can write better at the table,' he told her, taking out his notebook.

'You're taking notes?' She addressed the question to Neill.

'It's possible that a murder has been committed, ma'am,' he said heavily.

'I see.'

'You know?'

'I know some things.' She smiled gently: 'I assume others.'

'How much do you know?'

She looked at him intently.

'In Foodale,' she told him, 'we live very dull lives but I'm an elderly spinster with a vivid imagination. It's difficult to know where reality stops and fantasy begins sometimes—and one becomes forgetful in old age —but I'm aware of my limitations, although I don't always recognise them. It's impossible to say what I know, least of all to make a guess at what kind of information you want from me. If you were to ask me specific questions we would know where we are, or at least you

137

would start me—"point me" is the term, I believe—in the desired direction.'

Quinney wondered how much of this kind of thing the old man could take but in fact he acknowledged defeat immediately.

'Judy Scroop worked for you?'

'Yes.' Her eagerness to help was touching.

'How long had she worked for you?'

Her face fell.

'Dear me, I must think.' She started to calculate. 'Judy left school at fifteen and she is now twenty-five, so she must have worked for me at intervals for ten years.'

'You'd know her well then?'

She looked at him as if he'd suggested that she knew her monkey puzzle tree well.

'Do I? She was not a very good worker, missed the corners, you know, and the tops of wardrobes; one allowed her to prepare vegetables—she was no cook—but she *wasted* so much; however, as things are nowadays, with no girls going into service at all, we consider ourselves lucky to get anyone in Bardale. Annie is much better,' she added as an afterthought.

'Did she confide in you?'

'No, there would be no opportunity.'

'How's that, ma'am?'

'I have five acres of woodland and garden, inspector. I try to manage the woodland, to improve it for wildlife. One doesn't let it run riot. Properly looked after, you can increase the species on your land and still see that there's adequate food for them. We grow our own vegetables too, and all our fruit. I keep bees. Running five acres is a full-time job. Judy had to be left to do the housework alone and I doubt if both of us were ever idle at the same time. There was no opportunity for conversation,' she repeated. 'And what would we talk about?'

'Children?' Neill suggested.

'If Judy needed to consult anyone about her children she had her mother. In fact, so far as I know, the young Scroops are a very healthy family.'

'So you know nothing about her life outside this house,' Neill observed. 'Do you surmise anything?'

'No.' She was very firm. 'It would be unhealthy and unbecoming to speculate on other people's private lives if there were a tendency towards—' she looked away, searching for a word. 'Irregularity,' she said.

'In our position it's our duty to do so because until we know about her private life we can't hope to trace her movements, and if she's dead, we need that information to find her killer.'

Despite his style which he seemed to have caught from her, the last word was a nasty one for Foodale and Emily looked shocked.

'What do you want to know?' she asked.

'The first thing and the most essential is to know which men she was friendly with apart from Bill Lynch.'

'Why apart from him?'

'We have his name already.'

Emily thought for a moment.

'There was no one else,' she said.

'But if she didn't confide in you, ma'am, how can you be so sure?'

'I mean, no one so far as I know.'

'But there was someone last Saturday night—other than Bill Lynch. She went to Jagger's Barn to meet him, dropped her lipstick there, and was struck down as she entered the barn.'

'Yes,' Emily said, subdued. 'Mrs Stanton told me.'

So, thought Quinney, Neill was right, but how did

Judy get hold of the lipstick in the first place?

'What time did she leave here on Saturday?' Neill asked.

'About five o'clock.' She showed no surprise that he was so well-informed.

'Why did you send for her specially on Friday evening?'

'How curious,' she said in wonder. 'Who told you that?'

'Her mother.'

'Of course. But there was nothing sinister about it. There were visitors last weekend and I needed help.'

'You had visitors? When?'

'Mrs Stanton had guests.' She said it primly, reproving him for his inquisitiveness.

'May I ask when?'

'From Friday till Monday.'

'We weren't told—' He checked himself. 'Why did Judy Scroop work for you when it was Mrs Stanton had the work to do?'

'There were ducks to pluck. Judy was very good at preparing birds for the table. I killed them for Mrs Stanton's luncheon party on Sunday.'

'Who were the guests?'

'There was Dr Eden and his wife, Paul Trevena and myself.'

'Who is Paul Trevena?'

Emily was astonished.

'But surely you know he was here? Do you never go to the cinema? Mr Trevena is one of our leading film directors.'

'I see.'

Quinney kept his head down. They'd only been in Bardale twenty-four hours; perhaps there was some excuse for not knowing—but they'd seen most, if not all the people in the upper village and until this moment no one had thought to mention that there'd been a stranger in Foodale at the weekend.

'Is he making a film here?' Neill asked.

'I believe that's one of his interests in Bardale.'

It was as if ears had pricked in the kitchen.

'What are the others?'

'He collaborates with Mrs Stanton on big films: "for the wide screen" is the term, I understand. They're now working on a script about—no, I think I should leave you to ask them for the details. It may be confidential at this stage.'

'You say I should ask him. Is he staying there?'

'I don't know if he has come back.'

'You think he's likely to come back?'

She looked flustered.

'I had assumed. . . . You see, he's a close friend.'

'Of the family?'

'Yes, of the family.'

'Does Mr Stanton collaborate with him too?'

'Oh no. There's no question of *his* book being filmed.' She caught his look of surprise and hurried on: 'Mrs Stanton's books are written with filming in mind, or rather, the present one is. In fact, I believe it is being written as a *script*, and afterwards she may enlarge it into book form; I am not certain of the procedure but I do know that they work in very close co-operation, she and Mr Trevena. On the other hand, Mr Stanton's novel is a literary work: written to be *read*.'

'You might say then, that he writes for the satisfaction he gets out of writing, but she does it for the money.'

'No, I would not say that. Mrs Stanton takes great pleasure in writing, but you are correct in thinking she is a keen businesswoman. She frankly enjoys her success. No one can deny that she's a very wealthy woman

141

—and very happy too.' She darted a sharp glance at Neill. 'I am not an envious woman,' she went on. 'But, and partly because I do a little scribbling myself, I cannot help thinking that Mrs Stanton has a rather delightful life, you know?'

She beamed at them ingenuously.

'Money does help,' Neill sighed.

'Indeed, yes.' She looked round the kitchen with an abstracted air. 'I'm contented here. I don't have time to think—perhaps that's the trouble. If one had the money for a gardener now, or a good handyman.... I have always wanted to go to East Africa to see the big game before it's wiped out of existence, or orchids in the Amazon rain forest—or in Vietnam, but of course with defoliation.... I could just afford to do it but it's the difficulty and expense of getting a responsible person to look after the house and garden and the animals. One is so *tied.*'

'But if you have someone at home you can travel freely.'

'Yes. She's just had three months in Yugoslavia. Beautiful. And next year she plans to go to the Great Barrier Reef.'

'Pleasant for her husband.'

'She doesn't take him,' Emily said absently, looking out of the window.

'He must resent that.'

'He takes it in his stride. They are very modern.' Her gaze returned to him. 'They can lead separate lives without friction. Perhaps that is a good thing.' She sounded doubtful.

'—If you understand and appreciate the other person's way of life.'

'Yes.' She was incisive now. 'There must be understanding—and discretion.'

'Mrs Stanton is a discreet lady, would you say?'

'Indubitably.'

'But Mr Stanton impressed me as being rather too —"outgoing" I believe is the modern term. But he would surely want to keep up appearances?'

'Oh yes. He'd do his best.'

'You don't think much of him.'

'I didn't say that. It's merely that, in relation to his wife, who is a strong, dominant woman, he appears ineffectual and—er—vacillating. He needs looking after,' she smiled, 'which, presumably, is why he married Ruth Stanton. But he's a good father,' she added as if in extenuation. 'His daughter is the apple of his eye.'

'About Jagger's Barn,' Neill said.

She looked at him expectantly.

'When were you last there or in the vicinity?'

'On Friday afternoon.'

'Were the doors and gates closed?'

She thought for a moment.

'Yes.'

'Did you go inside?'

'No.'

'Why not?'

'Pointless,' she said shortly. 'There's nothing in the barn. There were barn owls but not now.' She smiled her sweet smile. 'May I offer you a cup of coffee, inspector?'

He accepted for both of them and she rose and filled an electric kettle. While she waited for it to boil Neill asked with apparently genuine curiosity:

'What's your opinion of this crime, ma'am?'

'Should I have one?'

'I think you have.'

'It was a sin—if murder has been done,' she qualified quickly. 'But all the same it was, if not excusable—it could never be that—it was predictable.'

'Meaning that eventually she was bound to run into trouble of her own making?'

'Inevitably. She went too far.'

'I'm afraid that's how it happens.' Neill agreed.

'She wasn't intelligent,' Emily said. 'Not defective, you understand, but although she had a fine instinct for your annoyance or pleasure, she had no long-term judgement, if you see what I mean. Judy was a child of nature and had no realisation of the consequences of her own actions.'

'She would break up families without realising what she was doing?'

'She broke up no families in Bardale,' Emily said. The kettle started to sing and she busied herself with cups. Suddenly she turned and faced them.

'I don't want to speak ill of the dead,' she said. 'But Ruth Stanton remarked only Sunday that there are certain people who are the typical murderee: they invite murder. You never met Judy but she flaunted her youth and her—appeal. I have spoken to her several times in an effort to—quieten her.'

'Did you have any success?'

'Ultimately—no.'

'There's one who reckons Judy Scroop is dead,' Quinney said, stopping the car in the lane. 'Past tense throughout.'

'Knows who did it too. *Reckons* she knows.' Neill corrected himself quickly. 'Did she find out the girl was meeting Stanton in the barn on Saturday nights and send for her specially to try to put a stop to it? That business about needing the girl to pluck ducks is a load of rubbish. These people don't leave their food till the last minute. We can take it those ducks were ordered well in advance, even fattened specially. But it's getting complicated—or is it? Who's this Trevena chap? Does he come in somehow?'

'Stanton's the favourite though,' Quinney said.

'We'll see. We know a sight more than we did last night.' He glanced in the direction of the barn but they were too low in the lane to see it. 'Depending on how it goes now, we might be taking a look at his garden quite soon.'

Chapter 10

'HE'S GONE TO Hernstone,' Ruth said. 'He'll be back soon.'

She reminded Quinney of Marilyn Hibbert when she'd told them that Michael was asleep. Ruth looked cool and elegant but she wasn't easy. She was wearing the cream suède suit today but it failed to do anything for her. She looked tired and her smile didn't reach her eyes.

She led them to the sitting room and asked if they could eat a sandwich with some coffee.

'I shouldn't think you'll get any lunch otherwise,' she said, but it was automatic hospitality, not sympathy for their job. She left them, presumably to order the food, for a vacuum cleaner which had been whining on the bedroom floor, stopped, and they heard voices.

Quinney looked round the room at the pictures: attracted and then annoyed by a reclining nude with limbs that seemed too long and a bit askew, puzzled by grey cottages against slate-grey hills in a place of honour beside the fireplace. He was squinting longsightedly at the backs of record sleeves when she returned, distractedly pushing back her hair. She sat down and watched them.

She was a crime writer, Quinney reasoned, she'd need every word, every gesture for raw material, but at the

146

moment she hadn't the air of an objective collector. It was a pity; she looked good when she was confident, as she'd been last night—until she'd started to wonder (hadn't she?) if her husband was giving little things of hers away, and what that could mean. It was fairly obvious that in the interval it had come to mean something significant to her.

'What have you found?' she asked Neill.

'Not much,' he said phlegmatically. 'It's her hair, of course, and her blood—on the cobbles too. It rained hard but there was plenty to identify as human, and to type, so there would have been a lot in the first place. I should qualify that, as you know: not *her* blood, but her *type*. They're searching for her body now,' he ended bleakly, glancing across the terrace.

'Buried?'

'Well,' he said with an approach to geniality. 'You're a crime writer, and a clever one, they tell me. What would you think? Underground or *in* the ground? In Styx Hole or the Outlands or the meadow by the bridge —or someone's garden?'

They watched closely and Quinney felt a wave of compassion. She looked stricken.

'You think it's one of us,' she whispered.

'Now, ma'am, that sounds like something out of a book.' Neill was enjoying himself and Quinney hated him. At that moment he wondered if he were cut out to be a policeman. It was his first big murder case.

'I don't see why you concentrate here,' she said.

Neill looked surprised.

'We're concentrating on the men who were intimate with her,' he said.

It was a gamble. Quinney wondered whether he'd ever see it come off quite like this again. She slumped in her chair and he noticed creases in the cream suit, a scuff on the ankle of an elegant boot; he saw that the skin on the back of her hands wasn't firm like a girl's. He looked at her face then and she was watching him, no, observing him. She smiled ruefully and he stared back without being aware of his bad manners.

'I'm afraid you're shocked,' she said to him as if Neill were not present.

The inspector rescued him, restoring the balance.

'Tell me what you did on Saturday evening,' he ordered, no longer genial.

'From six o'clock?'

'Go on.'

'I have to think.' She smiled deprecatingly. 'I don't think I did anything else but prepare dinner from six till seven-thirty. I can't imagine what time we left the table. Is it important?'

'It depends.'

She appeared to consider a rejoinder and rejected it.

'I had a guest for the weekend,' she went on. 'After dinner we discussed business until quite late and then we went to bed.'

'Now,' Neill said heavily, 'we'll need some times and some detail. We'll go back if you've no objection.'

She moistened her lips. Suddenly the door was pushed open and Annie Hibbert came in with a tray. It was so like the previous afternoon that the men were surprised to see her in a different dress. The woman put down the tray, ignored the detectives and addressed her employer:

'Is there anything else I can do, mum?'

'No, Annie, that will be all.'

'I'll get on with the vacuuming then. Give me a call if you needs me.'

She went out and left the door ajar. Quinney got up and closed it.

148

'What time do you think you finished your meal?' Neill asked.

'Perhaps we took an hour and a half. One really doesn't know the time if a party goes well and the conversation is interesting.'

'So we'll say you finished about nine o'clock.' Neill glanced at Quinney to make sure he was getting it. 'You didn't tell me who was eating with you.'

'Just the family: my husband and daughter, and Paul Trevena whom I'd brought down from London.'

He didn't comment on the name and she appeared surprised.

'So you left the table—and what did each of you do then?'

'We had coffee in here and then my husband went to his study to work—'

'How long before he left you?'

'About half an hour perhaps.'

'What did the rest of you do then?'

'Shortly after my husband left, my daughter went to bed—that would be about a quarter to ten, and that left Mr Trevena and myself in here, talking until midnight.'

She stopped and they all listened to the faint clicking of Quinney's biro.

'What time did your husband go to bed?' Neill resumed.

'I don't know. We have separate rooms.'

The pauses between questions were loaded.

'Was he still up when you went to bed?'

'Yes.'

'How do you know?'

'There was a light under the study door which is at the foot of the stairs.'

He was firing questions at her now.

'And you said goodnight to him?'

149

'No, I wouldn't dream of disturbing him when he's working.'

'Did anyone say goodnight to him?'

'No, and for the same reason.'

'So to your knowledge, no one saw your husband from about nine-thirty on Saturday evening until—when?'

'About ten o'clock on Sunday. I may have seen him about midnight,' she added casually.

Neill didn't look surprised.

'Would you explain that?' he asked.

She told him about the study curtain blowing in the breeze:

'The catch is defective unless the french window is bolted; he was in the woods—I thought I caught a glimpse of him—and he left the window ajar because both back and front doors would be bolted when we went to bed, and he wanted to make sure that he could get in again without knocking us up.'

'What time did he go out?'

'I have no idea.'

She was in full control of herself now and appeared totally unconcerned.

'Why was he out?'

'Oh, he was thinking: about the book he's writing. He'd been working for some hours, you see, and these rooms get stuffy, with central heating and draught proofing. We're always wandering round the grounds in the middle of the night when we're working.' She smiled. 'Even Miss Jebb was out that night, keeping foxes away from her hens. Of course, the horror of it is, we realise now, that amongst all the activity which we found amusing when we discussed it on Sunday, someone else was just across the ravine with Judy.'

'At midnight, ma'am?' Neill asked politely.

'How can anyone know what time she was killed—

150

even when you find the body?'

'You think the body will be found?'

'Of course. You came too quickly for the murderer to have time to dispose of it.'

'So where do you think it is?'

'Everyone guesses it's in Styx Hole.'

'You don't seem concerned about her being killed.'

'I'm concerned, but it happened three days ago. We've got over the first shock. Besides, you pointed out yourself that I'm a crime writer. I know Judy ran enormous risks; you know it too. It wasn't bound to happen but no one was surprised when it did.'

'You must have hated her.'

'Good gracious! Why do you say that?'

He didn't reply and she was forced to go on but she didn't seem worried about it.

'You mustn't judge us by the standards prevalent in the Street,' she said. 'They're very strict down there: Puritan. But in Foodale we're rather more—emancipated. Even Miss Jebb has a scientific approach to life rather than a moral one; perhaps that comes from generations of gentleman farmers in the background. I have no right to make conditions about my husband's personal life. Has anyone? I earn the money in this house. In order to do it I'm away a great deal and he looks after my home and our daughter. I don't neglect him but I do leave him free to lead his own life. That's the least I can do.'

'You have no objections as to who he picks up?'

'I'm not sure how much I could object in the circumstances,' she replied with a hint of dignity. 'But I knew Judy; she was a healthy girl and honest and she never presumed on the relationship.'

'Except to pilfer.'

'No,' Ruth said firmly. 'She didn't steal that lipstick.

My husband gave it to her because she "liked the shade".' She was quoting, appealing to them to share her amused annoyance. 'She was wearing my perfume on Saturday too,' she added wryly.

'Was your husband in the habit of giving her expensive presents which in fact belonged to you?'

'No, it only happened the two times.'

'Perhaps he needed to keep her quiet.'

'What for?'

'She could have been pregnant.'

'But there could be no proof as to who the father was.'

'If she threatened him—'

'How? Why? Judy was terribly easy-going and, quite frankly, inspector, she didn't take the initiative. She responded certainly, but fundamentally she didn't see men as individuals, only in the abstract—like food. She'd never have minded if a man wanted to throw her over; she didn't even recognise rejection. It was the men who approached her; she was merely, in the most basic sense, available. She was like a beautiful, flamboyant flower: if one fly went away, others came to take its place. Judy never threatened anyone in her life.'

'She was a threat,' Neill pressed.

'I assure you: it's impossible.'

'It's not impossible,' he said. 'It happened.'

'You're taking the same view as the Press,' she told him. 'It's not an informed view.'

'You gave Tom Pierce an interview.'

'Should I have refused?'

'Your husband did.'

'He had to go to Hernstone.'

'After Pierce arrived?'

'I can't remember. He wouldn't avoid the Press. He'll be home this afternoon when no doubt we'll have more visitors.'

Her co-operative mood was wearing thin.

'Let's get back to Saturday night,' Neill suggested. 'By my reckoning your guest was with you from about seven-thirty until midnight?'

'Yes.'

'You didn't leave him, or he leave you, at all during that time?'

'He probably went to the lavatory. I didn't keep a record.'

'Was he away for longer than five minutes at any time? Were you washing up, for instance?'

'No, I didn't wash up. He didn't leave me for longer than five minutes up till midnight.'

'When did you see him again after you went upstairs?'

She looked amused.

'At breakfast time on Sunday: about eight-thirty.'

'So he could have left the house after you'd gone to bed and visited Jagger's Barn.'

'He could have.'

She made no attempt to ridicule the suggestion.

The door opened and Ned Stanton looked in. He apologised but he didn't withdraw. Ruth looked at him calmly, then at Neill.

'If you've finished with me,' she said pointedly, 'I'll leave you with my husband.'

Neill thanked her grudgingly and she went out, passing her husband without touching him.

Ned came in and asked them if they would like a drink. When Neill refused, he poured himself a sherry and came to sit on the sofa.

'I'm sorry if I've kept you waiting,' he said. 'I had to go to town.'

'That's all right,' Neill told him. 'Your wife has been entertaining us.'

Ned didn't seem anxious although, with his watchful

153

eyes, he would never appear relaxed. Quinney studied the thin face and wondered what kind of mouth was concealed by the bushy beard.

Neill said smoothly:

'Tell us what you were doing on Saturday evening after six.'

He answered without hesitation:

'I worked in my study until seven-thirty, had dinner, then returned to work.'

'When did you leave it again?'

'Some time before my wife and Paul Trevena went to bed.'

'What time was that?'

'I don't know. I must have been out for an hour or so. When I went out, the light was still on in the sitting room but when I came back it was switched off and there were others on upstairs.'

'Where had you been?'

'In the garden.'

'Doing what?'

'Thinking about a problem I'd run up against in my work.'

'How long had you known Judy Scroop?'

There was a long pause during which Ned sat like a frozen animal. Quinney waited for the man to erupt in violence but when he spoke there was no sign of hostility nor of fear.

'Since we came here on our honeymoon about fifteen years ago.'

'How long have you been on intimate terms with her?'

'A long time. She first worked for us as a schoolgirl.'

'You mean—before she was fifteen?'

Ned looked uncomfortable.

'I shouldn't think so.' He was embarrassed. 'Why, she'd be the same age as Susan! Certainly not!'

'You mean you can't remember?'

He looked at them with surprise that seemed directed at himself.

'You know, I honestly can't remember.'

'But you might say she'd been your mistress for a number of years?'

'"Mistress" is too strong a term, but we have had an association for a number of years, yes.'

'How long has your wife known?'

'She didn't know.'

'She says she did.'

'She's saying that to protect me.'

'She thinks you did it then?'

'She says she doesn't but that's to my face. She believes I did it.'

'Did you?'

'No.'

'But you had a very good reason to do so.'

'No,' Ned said quietly. 'I had no motive.'

'We've been talking to your wife about the lipstick and scent that you gave the girl,' Neill said conversationally.

Ned's face changed. His eyes flashed.

'She could buy gallons of scent!' he protested. 'Why, she's got a flagon upstairs. And if that lipstick cost a pound, so what? She wouldn't notice it. Judy never had an expensive lipstick in her life and she liked the colour. The clothes my wife gives her are far more expensive; why make so much fuss about a lipstick?'

'The clothes are *given*; perhaps she objected to your attempts to redistribute her wealth,' Neill said slyly.

'It's unworthy of her. I can't think what kind of impression it made on you.'

'An impression of pride, and perhaps of proprietorship.'

Quinney was enthralled. This was a new Neill.

'You're quite right,' Ned acknowledged. 'She takes tremendous pride in her own success. It comes out at inopportune moments.' He stopped dead.

Neill returned his stare.

'Might she not have felt the same way towards your relationship with Judy Scroop?' he suggested. 'She could have had a proprietorial attitude towards her husband as well as her cosmetics. And the Scroop girl had been the cause of one woman leaving the village.'

'Who? Oh, Olive Lynch. My wife is a different calibre altogether. She'd never have left.'

'Quite. You would.'

'Me?'

'If it had come to a showdown you would have been forced to leave Bardale. Your wife might turn a blind eye to the occasional roll in the hay with the help but she'd never tolerate a liaison that became public, which it could have done if Brenda Scroop put her daughter up to trying to obtain a paternity order against you.'

'She could never have proved it.'

Neill stared at him thoughtfully. Quinney coughed. The sad gaze came round to him. Neill nodded. Ned's eyes shifted to the sergeant.

'This business of Mrs Stanton and Paul Trevena,' Quinney began, noting a flicker of apprehension appear in Stanton's eyes. 'You wouldn't want a divorce, of course.'

Ned studied the fire. Neill was expressionless.

'My wife hadn't asked me for a divorce,' Ned said carefully.

'But you knew she was likely to.'

'The thought never crossed my mind. We were all happy as we were.'

'Someone wasn't happy as they were,' Quinney observed. 'Someone had a very great deal to lose last Saturday night. He killed to preserve it.'

'No. You think someone's been killed, but you haven't got a body.'

'Do I have to remind you of murder convictions where the body has never been found?' Neill asked.

'There must be circumstantial evidence.'

'There must be evidence,' Neill corrected. 'We intend to get it. You have no objection to us looking round your garden, I trust.'

Ned's eyes sparkled.

'None at all.'

That's that, Quinney thought with satisfaction; she's down Styx Hole.

PART III

Chapter 11

THE STOUT MAN looked like Humpty Dumpty in a raincoat. He even had a bow tie. He prodded the rose bed with a long stick. She saw Renishaw shake his head and point to soil a few feet away where she had been weeding. She watched the stick sink in the rich loam, saw them draw together, concentrating on the lack of resistance, on the possibility that Judy Scroop might be lying a few feet below the surface. Unaware of what she was doing, she clutched the heavy curtains, and a cool hand was placed on hers.

'Careful now,' Annie warned. 'You'll have them drapes down.'

The older woman glanced carelessly out of the window as she turned her employer gently and pushed her towards the bed.

'It's not true, is it?' Ruth whispered. 'She's not there?'

'No, she's not there. Don't you fret yourself; they'll never find her.'

Annie took a cup of tea from the bedside table and offered it.

'God, Annie! You've put sugar in it!'

'I know. Drink it.'

Ruth drank obediently, her eyes still wide and blank with shock.

'There isn't any capital punishment, is there?' she pleaded.

'Not no more,' Annie assured her. 'But you got no cause to worry. They'll let him go after a while. They'll ask him a lot of questions, give him a shaking up, and let un go.'

'Don't joke, Annie.'

'I'm not joking. Drink your tea. He'll be back here in a day or two and let's hope he'll have learned his lesson this time.'

'What lesson?'

'Why, to stop running after tramps like her. Although, give him his due, it were only the one, but he had to pick the dirtiest little cat in the dale.'

'Annie!' If one could be shocked out of shock, this was it. 'She wasn't as bad as that. She never made trouble.'

'Never made trouble! Look at you now. Isn't that all along o' that whore? Bardale was never the same since they come here, her and that mother. They've upset every family in the dale one time or another.'

Annie stalked to the window and stood there conspicuously, staring down at the searchers.

'Look at that now,' she flung over her shoulder, pointing. 'Digging up your rose beds!'

Ruth pressed a hand against her mouth, trying to quell the rising hysteria. She took deep breaths and made an effort to think.

'Did you say everyone's suffered from Judy?' she asked.

'Shouldn't be surprised.'

'It seems rather unfair of the police to pick on Mr Stanton then.'

'Well,' Annie reiterated, 'you got no cause for alarm 'bout *them*.' She nodded towards the garden. 'Here's

162

Susan coming up the drive; I'll go down and get her tea.'

'Sue! She mustn't see—'

Ruth flung herself towards the door and rushed downstairs, realising as she did so that Susan would have seen them already. She stopped in the ground floor passage, at a loss. The back door slammed and she went slowly towards the kitchen.

'Hello, Mum,' Susan said, and looked at her searchingly. 'You need a cup of tea. Where's Annie?' The woman had followed Ruth downstairs. 'There you are. Make us a fresh pot, Annie; I need one too. Bet we all do.'

'Who told you?' Ruth asked weakly.

The girl ticked names off on her fingers.

'Henry Raven, Mrs Padley, and a very young police cadet by Styx Hole who hadn't been briefed on the background and so didn't know who I was.'

'How much do you know?' Ruth sat down heavily while Annie set out cups.

'Everything,' Susan said gravely and glanced at Annie's back as she went to the fridge. 'As much as anyone, I suppose,' she corrected herself. 'You see, Mum, Bardale treats girls of fourteen as adults.'

Ruth started to say dryly that this was obvious when there was a peremptory knock and the outer door opened.

'Hello, my loves,' Paul Trevena said, and Ruth, after the first wild start of recognition, burst into tears.

'Oh Christ, darling!' Paul said.

'It's all right,' Susan assured him. 'It's the shock. They've taken Ned for questioning. When she gets over this, take her away and she can pour it all out to you. No, leave her a moment—' as he moved towards Ruth, '—go and wait in the sitting room. She'll join you.'

Paul peered at her quizzically as she pushed him out of the kitchen.

163

'You all right?'

She nodded impatiently and turned back to her mother. Quickly and practically the girl and the woman set things to rights: pouring out tea and a glass of brandy, Susan fetching a wet sponge and several large handkerchiefs.

'My God,' Ruth said between sobs, lifting her head. 'Can it get any worse?'

'You don't mean Paul's arrival makes it worse?' Susan asked, but she didn't wait for an answer. 'Do you feel up to telling him?'

'Telling him what?'

'Everything.' She regarded her mother doubtfully.

'Should she?' Annie asked.

'Yes,' Susan said. 'She has to.'

'You've taken charge,' Ruth observed with a weak smile.

'I'm a sort of liaison officer,' the girl said. 'Half-Bardale, half-incomer: a foot in each camp.'

'Did you really mean you know everything that's going on?' Ruth asked in wonder but with a dawning horror in her eyes.

'Of course not, Mum. You know how I exaggerate. But you can stop worrying about Ned.'

'I told her that,' Annie said.

Susan glanced at the woman.

'What about Michael?' she asked.

'That's all right. A man come over and said he was at the club in Sheffield. He recognised our Michael. And that Hughie Blount and the others stand by him.'

The girl nodded.

'You see,' she turned to Ruth, 'there's no body and there's nothing to tie her death to any of us.'

'Is that fact or wishful thinking?'

'It's fact, Mum.'

'I don't know what's going on,' she confessed to Paul after she'd poured out the story of what had happened since he left on Monday morning. 'Sue and Annie seem to know everything between them, and the police know something, although it doesn't seem to be the same things. There's that horrible soft man in the raincoat, and Renishaw—who suddenly becomes terrifying because he's so thorough; they're poking in the flower beds and going through the wood, and there's Ned taken away—and Neill went with him. That means Neill thinks it's Ned, and although he told me he didn't kill her, at least, I think he said he didn't, it looks so black for him.'

'What do you mean: you *think* he told you he didn't do it?' Paul asked.

'Yes, it's crazy, isn't it? Things are so involved, you see. He had to tell me the truth when I tackled him about the lipstick—I'd lost other odd things too, nothing valuable, it was as if a magpie was pilfering; didn't you notice the French perfume on her on Saturday? I'd guessed while I was abroad. Obviously he didn't want me home at the particular moment that I phoned from Ljubljana and I thought then that if it had been anyone else, the trouble would have been a woman, but with Ned I blocked it out and pretended to believe his story when I got home about his being mixed up in some conservation campaign which was demanding all his attention and making him irritable. In fact, when I phoned from Yugoslavia, Judy had just walked out (she hated men being serious about her) and he was trying to make her come back. He was infatuated with her; it's pitiful, isn't it?'

'Did he tell you all this?'

'Yes, on Monday evening, after the police had gone. He didn't kill Judy because she was pestering him, but because her exploits drove him mad with jealousy.'

'My dear girl!'

He got up and poured out a large brandy, and sherry for himself.

'Now drink this and let's try to look at this thing objectively. It was fortunate I came,' he added smugly. 'Much as I dislike Ned, I have an innate objection to seeing anyone's grave dug quite so effectively.'

'What have I done?'

'Oh, it doesn't matter what you've said to me; I'm wondering how much of this you've told the police.'

'None of it. But you can see why it happened. You remember saying I had a blind spot regarding Ned?'

'I wasn't thinking of his sex life so much as his professional pride.'

'Masculine pride,' she corrected. 'Resentment over my being the bread-winner and buying his cars: keeping him. Judy was his way of rebellion. He told me so, not in so many words, but it all came out.'

'I don't believe it.'

'Does everyone have to cast doubt on every statement?' She was furiously angry. 'The police don't believe a word one says, and now you. I'm surrounded by lies.'

'You're lying yourself.'

'I'm not!'

'You're lying to the police, trying to protect Ned. You never knew that he was meeting Judy at Jagger's. Did he tell the police voluntarily that he was meeting her up there?' he asked curiously.

'They knew already, when they came here the second time.' She started to repeat Neill's answer when she'd asked why the police were concentrating on Foodale, on Heathens' Low, but she faltered. 'They *didn't* know,' she breathed. 'It was a bluff.'

They were silent for a moment.

'I know why I fell for it,' she went on. 'Because I'd conditioned myself to thinking that this was the crucial interview, that I had to cover for Ned, but until that point I wasn't sure where I was, and I was terrified. When Neill said they were concentrating on the men who'd been intimate with Judy, I thought—what he intended me to think.' She smiled wryly. 'That remark switched me on but my reaction told them that Ned was one of the intimates, didn't it?'

'They'd have found out.' He was reassuring. 'But it's two different things, don't you see: a roll in the hay isn't a love affair. Why should he kill her? You wouldn't have minded if you'd known—would you?'

She thought about this.

'No, I wouldn't have minded. I'm not possessive about Ned.'

'He's intelligent enough to know that. Ned *is* intelligent.' He emphasised the point. 'You didn't see him in the garden after you'd gone to bed on Saturday, did you?'

'I could have done.' She was evasive.

He glanced at her but didn't comment.

'Do you really think he did it?'

She looked at him helplessly.

'There's all Saturday night to account for,' she pointed out. 'And the study window was open—and he did a lot of caving here when he was young. He'd know where to put the body where it wouldn't be found. You see, Susan and Annie keep stressing that the body will never be found.'

His face changed.

'Come away with me. Come back to London,' he said urgently.

'Darling! How could I leave him now—and Susan?'

'Bring her, of course; she shouldn't be here any more than you. What right has he to expect you to stay? He's using you, can't you see that? He's behaved despicably, even if he isn't a murderer; it's a sordid business and he's involved you to the hilt. I won't have you a party to all this.'

'Paul, do you realise that if we had capital punishment, his life would be at stake?'

'Oh, come off it, ducky! Let's give the melodrama a miss. He's getting no more than he deserves.'

'Curiously enough, that's just what Annie said.'

'And doesn't that rile you: to know the Street is passing judgement on your husband's *affaire de coeur?*' His tone implied that the affair was anything but romantic. 'Come on, we can be at the flat tonight—Susan too.' He gripped the arms of his chair as if he were ready to leave at that moment.

'I won't go while he's being questioned,' she said stubbornly.

'For Heavens' sake! Would you come if they released him?'

She hesitated.

'Not while he needs me. It's unfair, darling; you can't mix *us* with this other thing. They're separate. I must stand by Ned.'

'How corny can you get?'

'Isn't it odd,' she asked in tragic bewilderment, 'how terribly dramatic one sounds at the most heartrending moments?'

He opened his mouth to protest and shut it again. The telephone was ringing. They waited, heard Annie's voice, heard her say:

'She went out. Can I take a message?'

The receiver was replaced and there was a knock at the sitting room door.

'It was the *Express*,' Annie said. 'I told un you'd gone out. Is that all right?'

'Thank you, Annie. Just go on telling them I'm out, will you?'

'They'll get to you, to us, eventually,' he said, when the woman had gone back to the kitchen.

'The *Graphic* was here this morning.'

'What did you tell them?'

'I just gave him the background: dales talk. Ned slipped out of the back door and stayed away for an hour or two. He came back just in time to catch the police,' she said bitterly. 'Although I suppose that, as things were going, they'd have waited here until he showed up. By the way, Neill suggested you could have killed Judy. You slept alone. You have no alibi.'

He smiled absently.

'I could lay a false trail and get Ned off the hook,' he said. His eyes sharpened. 'Lay a false trail,' he repeated, staring at her. 'Is that what *he's* doing? To protect someone?'

She said nothing but waited. She was almost exhausted.

'Who?' he asked himself. 'Ned's a downy bird, not much human feeling there—' She frowned in protest but he ignored her. '—He's an idealist.... John Eden's similar, really. Would Ned protect John, or is that too individualistic? Ned likes causes. What was the motive for killing Judy?'

He wasn't really asking her but she answered.

'Blackmail?'

He stared at her in astonishment.

'I know it's stupid,' she agreed. 'But that could be the way the police are looking at it. Judy wanted to settle down, so she needed a husband. She was simple enough to think that Heathens' belonged to Ned. He'd imply

169

that, you know. Men do that kind of thing. He was frightened and held out against her. They quarrelled and he hit her. He didn't mean to hit so hard.'

'Are you saying what happened?' He glared at her.

'No, what they suspect happened. It could have been like that, unfortunately. Ned's a type. That's how the type reacts.'

'You and your blind spot! It's absolutely senseless. That isn't Ned at all. He's protecting someone else.'

She watched him carefully.

'It's all talk,' she said. 'We could spend days arguing over this. It hinges on people's personalities.'

'We can do more than talk. If Ned's protecting someone, we can find out whom. That would put him in the clear. Would you come back to London with me then?'

'Yes.'

They regarded each other steadily.

'I see,' he said. 'We both want the same thing for different reasons. You want Ned cleared for some irrelevant principle like marital duty or loyalty; I want him in the clear just so that I can get you away. I know you won't rat on it though. Do you love him?'

'That has nothing to do with it,' she said equably. 'But I have great faith in you. If anyone can find out who killed her, you will.'

He nodded, then his mouth twitched in a mischievous grin.

'I'll turn Bardale upside down—discreetly, of course. I'll find out who got Judy Scroop *and* where they put her if it's the last thing I do.'

Chapter 12

'HELLO,' LAURA SAID carefully. 'Come in.'

She peered out at the dusky evening.

'Are you alone?'

'Quite alone,' Paul told her. 'Where's John?'

'At the Woman. Haven't you heard?'

'I've heard a great deal, but the Woman seems something new. Don't tell me they've found Judy Scroop in the potato patch after all?'

'You will have your little joke,' she said unhappily, leading him to the sitting room. The beat of pop music from behind closed doors suggested that the boys were doing their homework. 'Just as it happens,' she continued, handing him a sherry, 'Brenda thought along the same lines. It took her a long time to work out why the police wanted Judy's hair brush, poor thing. And I suppose no one had the heart to tell her about the blood on the barn door—' She stopped and peered at him. 'I take it you have come from Heathens' and you've been briefed?' He nodded. She went on: 'Brenda found out what was happening eventually (I expect the Press told her), had a fit of hysterics, and John put her under sedation. The children were sent to Bull Low and he got a woman to sit with her. This all happened this morning. When Brenda woke up she rushed out of the house and across the yard to the Woman and attacked Bill Lynch with a branding iron.'

'With *what*?'

'You must have seen it: hanging on the wall of the bar. The other woman had followed and there was a policeman in the bar and they managed to get Brenda back to the cottage and to send for John. But Lynch has had a stroke. The police traced Olive to Bowes and they've sent for her.'

'Bowes? Where's that?'

'Somewhere on the northern Pennines. Poor Bill, imagine thinking of him as a multiple murderer! He was probably enjoying the notoriety but it backfired. He lived too near the mother of one of the supposed victims.'

'It's not "supposed" for Judy,' he pointed out. 'So Bill Lynch is in the clear?'

'There can't be any doubt about it. He was in very poor shape physically, and the strain of humping her body about, let alone the excitement of the actual murder, would have prostrated him. That's what John says. He couldn't have done it. Tell me,' she went on more warmly, 'how is Ruth bearing up?'

'You know Ned's been taken away?'

'Yes. Emily rang.'

'Emily Jebb? How does she know? Never mind. Ruth's got over the shock and she's taking it very well, considering.'

'Ned's been so *stupid*, but I really can't see him hitting Judy over the head, can you?'

'Why not?'

'Oh, Paul! Ned's a cold fish. Do you think he ever felt passion for anyone—or anything other than cleaning up the Trent or banning supersonics?'

'Ned's a great man for causes,' he agreed. 'Perhaps he

felt that if Judy wouldn't be sterilised she should be eliminated.'

Laura smiled wryly.

'It used to drive John up the wall, but then he said Bardale was being depopulated all the time and the kids would probably become farm labourers and stay here, and we could employ the girls in the houses, so really Judy was only restoring the balance. I expect that was just theorising but since you couldn't do anything about her, you had to accept the situation and find a bright side.'

'Good for you, but you can be more objective than most. You haven't got the police poking about in your flower beds.'

'No! Are they doing that at Heathens'? But that's ridiculous. Even the police can't believe Ned brought her back and buried her in the garden. Why, all the household would have to be in on the conspiracy: Ruth, Susan, and you too.'

'They've got to look everywhere; they're only digging where there's newly turned earth.'

She giggled wildly.

'I've had it then. I set out a bed of aquilegias this afternoon. Do you think they'll replace the plants?'

'You're all right,' he said airily. 'John's got an alibi.'

She said nothing. She was frowning.

'He must have,' he protested as if her silence contradicted him.

'It was the night Dora Bagshawe had her third,' she said. 'Up at Paradise. He woke me when he came in.' She stood up and took his empty glass. 'How is Susan taking it?' she asked, too brightly.

Their attempts to chat proved artificial and, after a quarter of an hour, both of them welcomed the appearance of John Eden. He had come straight from the

Street and he looked haggard. Over a whisky he told them that Olive had returned—in a chauffeur-driven Rolls, which put her down and departed mysteriously —but that Lynch was partially paralysed.

'All because of an illusion,' Laura murmured.

John stared at her, apparently too tired to understand. She was instantly full of consternation.

'I'm so sorry, my dear! You're exhausted and I'm so woolly! I meant that stupid business of Olive being in the potato patch, then Judy—oh really, it's so fantastic now, isn't it? But Brenda believed it and she's responsible for the present situation.'

'You mean his illness? She only precipitated it. He was sinking a fair quantity of brandy every day. It would have happened quite soon without Brenda's intervention; a quarrel with a customer, a bout of bad temper, even frustration, could have brought it on.'

'What about Olive?' Paul asked, and at that moment a telephone started to ring. Laura went out to answer it.

John looked at him with some return of animation now that he was sitting down and the whisky was taking effect.

'What about her?'

'How does she seem? Guilty, astonished at events, angry?'

The doctor studied his hands, then his visitor. He frowned.

'I was concentrating on Lynch and on giving her directions for nursing him, then I had to make sure the constable would be handy in case Brenda came back, although I think I've convinced her now that Lynch couldn't have been in any way responsible for Judy's death. These—tasks—claimed all my attention. On reflection, Olive was no different from what she was before, when she lived here. She didn't seem upset.

Perhaps she accepted the situation.'

'You mean she accepted the murder?'

John explored this possibility in silence. At length he said:

'Presumably she knew something about it from the radio but she wouldn't feel concerned. She's a shrewd woman and once she'd decided that Lynch wasn't, or couldn't be involved, because of his condition, she'd concentrate on the immediate problems: his illness, organising the nursing, running the business. She's very practical and not in the least troubled by atmosphere. If she considered the murder at all it would be in relation to its attraction for the Press and weekend tourists.'

He said this without a trace of malice. It was a fact.

In the silence that followed Paul could distinguish the faint background noise of the boys' transistor and the sound of Laura replacing the telephone receiver. Her heels clicked on the parquet.

'That was Ruth,' she told them, coming back. She looked at Paul doubtfully. 'She wants me to go over.'

John rose.

'Perhaps I should—'

'No, I asked specifically. She doesn't want anything, just to chat. You stay here, darling, and have an early night. You're worn out.' This time there was no mistaking the look she directed at Paul but he was studying a colourful abstract hanging above his chair and was quite oblivious.

When she'd gone they sat down again. If John resented Paul's presence he didn't show it. Instead he inspected his visitor with interest but Paul, waiting for the other to speak first, remained stubbornly silent.

'Why do you want to see me?' John asked at last, and the other released his breath in a sigh.

'I want information.'

'About Judy?'

'About her, and others, and about her death.'

'Why?'

This time it was Paul's turn to be silent, marshalling his thoughts. Bardale and its associates had always been aware that John Eden was direct; that such directness demanded honesty in return; they'd never had cause to anticipate that a situation involving the most basic principles would accentuate such demands. Suddenly Paul realised that he'd jumped the gun and it was too late to go back. But the room was cosy and the drink soothing; in the background two youngsters did their homework to the accompaniment of pop. If John were a killer then he must be a maniac to attempt anything in the present circumstances. Paul stared at him frankly, speculating. His host's eyes showed curiosity, not calculation; they were neither manic nor fanatic. Paul plunged, trusting that what he said wouldn't go beyond that room.

'I'm in love with Ruth and I want to marry her. There's nothing between her and Ned, and she'd leave him tonight, except that he's suspected of killing Judy; he could even be charged by this time. I'm certain he didn't do it, I know Ruth would like to believe he didn't, but the point is the police won't let him go till they've got someone better. While he's suspected, Ruth will stay here. If he's safe back at Heathens' and someone else is in his place, she'll come away with me.'

Typically, John ignored the less important moral angle.

'So you're determined to find another person to take his place,' he commented.

'No, I'm looking for the murderer.'

'What makes you think it isn't Ned?'

'One, he had no motive. Two, he worked too hard

to incriminate himself. Three, he couldn't have disposed of the body; and four, it's out of character. He isn't a man given to violent outbursts; just the opposite, in fact.'

John regarded him thoughtfully, and without any effort went back over the four points, but slowly:

'First, as to motive: there was security. Ned needs that no less than other men. He might kill for it, not passionately, but cold-bloodedly, if it were threatened—as it might have been—by Judy. Secondly, how do you know he worked to incriminate himself? It might have been clever questioning that did it, not voluntary confession. Three: until the body is found, no one knows how difficult—or simple—it was to dispose of. As for his character, that comes under motive. He is curiously amoral. Has it ever occurred to you that Ned's conservationist activities are a form of anarchy? He's not party-political; he's against any party or all parties because they're all orientated in favour of a consumer society which, in his book, is the source of all pollution, from noise to delinquency. Yet Ned is almost totally dependent on his creature comforts, provided by the consumer society via the mass media—and via Ruth. This dependence on society associated with his rejection of it must build up enormous pressures.'

'Which could result in violence?'

'I don't know. I've drawn his character as I see it, as you must see it. Did you ever meet anyone who took luxury more for granted? Can you imagine him living on a subsistence income?'

'I don't see how such pressures could result in him hitting a girl even if he didn't intend to hit so hard.'

'To preserve his way of life. We all want to do that if we've arrived at a level we find worth preserving. I have, for instance.'

177

He appeared to be waiting. Paul picked up his cue with a kind of academic curiosity.

'So what is your alibi?'

'I have none.'

'I'm starting to get an inkling of what this is about,' Paul said. 'Go on; I shall try to break your non-alibi.'

John recited with a trace of amusement:

'I was called out to Dora Bagshawe at Paradise Farm at about nine-thirty and there was some difficulty with the birth but I left there at about midnight. I stopped on Bardale Bank for quite a time, nearly an hour, I imagine. I reached home about one in the morning. Laura didn't wake up. I have no alibi from about midnight until seven in the morning when Christopher and I met in the kitchen.'

'Laura says you woke her when you came in.'

John smiled.

'We're a happy family,' he said simply.

'You shouldn't have said that. It invalidates any motive.'

'On the contrary, my family comes first with me.'

'But not your personal security.'

John spread his hands helplessly.

'No.'

'You capitulate?'

'Not at all. There could be other motives. And I have no alibi.'

'Ah, yes. You left Paradise (doesn't that sound delightful?) at midnight and you arrived home at one. Where did you stop, and why?'

'About halfway down the Bank, in that lay-by above the water meadows. I had time for two leisurely cigarettes.'

'You don't smoke.'

'It's one of my failings—which I trust you not to

178

divulge. Very occasionally I smoke: in the open air where the smoke won't cling and give me away. I'd had a hard day last Saturday, and a harder hour or two immediately before. When I reached the lay-by, I got out with my cushion and my padded anorak and I sat on the wall up there and listened to the foxes. It seemed at the time to be a beautiful night. I hope,' he added, his voice changing perceptibly, 'that Judy didn't suffer.'

'You could no more convince the police that you had a hand in it than you can me.'

The doctor made no comment on this.

'What do you propose to do?' he asked.

'Where do you stand?'

'Yes,' John Eden said. 'You must understand that part. You see, we have no church and no priest in the dale, and some of us need a confidant other than a spouse. In the nature of my profession I'm told confidences which don't relate to people's physical well-being. Those are inviolate.'

'I was thinking it was something like this.'

'So I can give you no positive help.'

'You know who did it?'

'I don't know.'

'You can guess.'

The doctor put a log on the fire and watched the bark catch and spit tiny sparks.

'A number of people had motives,' he admitted. 'It wasn't what is known as a motiveless murder. But there's no one who is bad in Bardale; weak, some of them, but not wicked. Someone thought they had justification in killing Judy Scroop.'

'How did they dispose of the body?'

John nodded as if in agreement.

'I've thought about that. I would say Styx Hole. There were no police about as I came home so I would say the search party has come out. It would take days to search that place properly, and they've got to do the sump. Some of it's unexplored. The police may be caving experts but I doubt if they're of the same calibre as pioneers. It's quite astonishing the places boys can get to that adults, even experts, can't. You know, it's only recently that climbers have discovered the cliffs here but Joe Hibbert, and Henry Raven too, scrambled about all over these faces when they were young. They went underground too. I should think every man in Bardale knows Styx well, perhaps even the unexplored parts.'

'There aren't many men in the Street and Foodale,' Paul pointed out. 'Excluding you, Ned, Henry Raven and Bill Lynch, there are three. I'd be inclined to exclude old Padley as well. That leaves the Hibberts, father and son.'

The words hung in the air. John rose, took his guest's glass in silence, and filled it. Having returned it, he walked to the window and pulled back the curtains. Paul watched the thin shoulders and the back of the dark head, wondering if it was possible that his search could end so suddenly, or at least that the end would be shown him at this moment; knowing that something had to be said to resolve the situation, feeling, despite himself, awed and a little frightened. And the doctor confirmed this feeling. He turned and came back to his chair beside the fire. His face was set. He sat down and regarded Paul, and through the grimness the latter caught a spark of sympathy. For himself, or others, or all of them?

'Bardale is ingrown,' the doctor told him. 'You can see the analogy in the Street and those little parlours shadowed by the cliffs across the road. It's the same at the back, perhaps worse. There are paved yards giving on the river which isn't very deep, but dark and quite silent. In the past they built walls, less to keep the children safe than to shut off the water, but it's still there, across the wall. The river and the cliffs don't make for healthy minds except with game old extroverts like Henry Raven and the Padleys.

'I don't suppose that basically Bardale is different from any other remote village in England; its people may be a bit more arthritic and mentally unstable, but all these aspects add up to a community that isn't superficially a closed one—after all, they accepted incomers without hostility: the Scroops and the Lynches, Ruth, Marilyn Hibbert, us, they accepted them originally—but when someone became a threat, then they closed in on themselves like cattle, with the horns outside.'

He paused to reflect.

'Judy was a threat for a long time,' Paul said softly.

'Judy? I was thinking of the police as the ultimate threat. But Judy—yes. Most murders are the result of two main factors. Judy's anti-social behaviour had come to be resented by someone so much that only murder could resolve the situation. The girl was anti-social in the strictest sense although the ostensible motive would be far more personal, of course. Basically, it's anthropological,' he murmured.

'Oh, come now. You're saying someone killed her to protect the village?' Paul protested.

'No—although you might say that society will always act against its deviants, whatever tool is used. Specifically, someone took the law into their own hands because Judy became a personal threat. It was afterwards that the village went on the defensive.'

'Meaning they're completely lawless, like Ned Stanton.'

'No, they recognise a law but it's older than our social

laws. And remember that peasants from time immemorial have taken great pleasure in outwitting the established order. It starts with poaching the squire's pheasants. Once murder is done, I doubt if your poacher-peasant would have any qualms about being an accomplice after the fact. And don't forget that most of Bardale is related. I would say that Ned Stanton is enjoying himself.'

'I appreciate your analysis of Bardale,' Paul said. 'But we have to come back to individuals, don't we? Judy wasn't abstract but a person, and she wasn't killed by an anthropological principle that refuses to accept deviants, but by a man. Presumably by Michael Hibbert, but he's got a cast-iron alibi.'

'If you hound Michael Hibbert,' the doctor said intensely, 'you will have to answer for the consequences. The boy's weak but he's fighting to get back on an even keel. With his family to help him he may make it. Underneath that selfishness there's a lot of insecurity. I think he'll lose that with Marilyn. If the police come after him, he's going to feel victimised, and with good cause. He was the first person in the Street that they went to.'

'You don't think he did it?'

'Don't hound him,' John Eden said. 'That's a warning. That boy must be left alone.'

'Is it Joe then?'

'Joe didn't kill her,' John said with finality.

Chapter 13

'WHAT'S THE SUMP?' Paul asked, stroking the tortoiseshell queen and sipping Emily's elderberry wine
appreciatively.

'The sump? On a car?'

She peered at him through her steel-rimmed spectacles.

'The sump in Styx Hole.'

'I see.... It's an underground passage that's completely flooded: the roof is underwater. It's about two
hundred feet long. Why do you ask?'

He looked at her steadily.

'I'm wondering where the body is.'

'Not in the sump,' Emily said firmly. 'They went
down with breathing apparatus this afternoon. The sump
would be the first place to look, not because you could
hide a body there, but simply because several have
turned up in it. They were accidents, of course.'

'Where is the second most likely place to look?'

'Styx Hole has innumerable ramifications. There is
the Old Series which is the part that's been explored,
and the New Series, which lies through the sump and
has only been entered, I think, twice, by two men. One
was a caving instructor who managed to get through the
passage during an exceptional drought; the other was a
rescuer who went in to retrieve a body. In fact, he

continued past the body and came out in the New Series but in the circumstances he had no chance to explore and had to return. I assume no one has followed him because it is too difficult and dangerous—which is, of course, why people are drowned there. Why are you particularly interested in finding the body?'

'Simply because if we found her we should know how she was killed and, possibly, who killed her.'

'You don't believe it's Ned.'

'No. Do you?'

'It would be wiser to let sleeping dogs lie.'

'I think it's Michael Hibbert,' he said.

Emily smiled pleasantly.

'It wasn't Michael,' she assured him. 'He has an alibi.' She twinkled at him. 'And only a rich London gang could afford to bribe so many witnesses in a murder case. Michael is completely innocent, my dear, you have my word for that, and you know I don't lie.'

He did know it.

'And his father?'

'Hibbert kills only villains like crows. You know Joe. Who have you been listening to?'

'I've been talking to John Eden.'

'And who does he favour?'

'He's been trying to convince me that he did it himself, and failing miserably.'

'Yes,' she said thoughtfully. 'He would. Leave it alone, Paul. She's dead now, and no amount of ferreting in people's lives is going to bring her back.'

'Do you condone it?'

'No, but it's happened. We have to accept it.'

'And accept that there's a murderer among us?'

'*Us,* my dear. Not you. You are on the outside.'

'Meaning I'm interfering.'

'It's not your business.'

184

He stared at her. She was quite serious. He didn't feel capable of the effort to establish his right of inquiry into the murder of any citizen, let alone this one; he felt that for one evening he'd revealed enough of affairs which involved Ruth as well as himself. Instead he said:

'So Michael is completely trustworthy?'

'Not completely,' she said dryly. 'But he isn't involved in Judy's death, so you must leave him alone.'

'What do you think of Padley?' he asked.

'*Padley?* In what connection?'

'As a murderer.'

'My dear man, you're being ridiculous. You might as well suggest Henry Raven; Padley had as little interest in Judy.'

'Yes, I thought it was scraping the bottom of the barrel,' he admitted in some embarrassment. 'But he was the only one left, you see. However, I'm glad you've satisfied me regarding Michael Hibbert; now I feel free to pursue another line of inquiry.'

After the sherry at Yaffles, Emily's elderberry wine left him feeling elated. He said goodnight to the old lady, assuring her that he was going back to keep Ruth company but neglecting to mention that Laura was at Heathens' Low. He did turn up Ruth's drive when he came to it, but he went to his car, not the house.

The Bentley crept down the drive and nosed into the lane. Lights gleamed above him in the three Foodale houses, giving no hint of the conversations that might be in progress, of confidences being exchanged behind drawn curtains.

At the upper bridge he wondered if he should take a look at Styx Hole, but he thought the Bentley would be too conspicuous parked here, and he continued down the Street to turn in at the Quiet Woman.

'Mr Trevena!' The metallic accents recalled a time when Bardale was only a sleepy village with a cave for its sole attraction.

Olive Lynch had changed. She had bleached her hair and she was wearing an ivory dress that was a shade too long and strung with gilt chains. He could smell Patou's *Joy*. Her sharp rodent face was lit by a professional smile. The only other people in the bar were two lads probably from Bull Low and a middle-aged man who looked like a policeman.

'How's Bill?' Paul asked, feeling sudden sympathy for a man who had reaped far more than he deserved from one small wild oat, or was it a dragon's tooth?

He found a whisky in his hand and Olive was saying:

'He's sleeping. He can't say anything yet. The doctor says it's only to be expected. He'd been drinking rather more than was good for him with his blood pressure and then the shock—' She paused significantly. Paul murmured condolences.

'I'm coping,' she responded. 'Lily Raven's sitting with him at the moment. You've had your share of excitement in Foodale,' she added pointedly, as if to remind him that scandalous behaviour wasn't confined to the Woman.

He eyed her thoughtfully, downed his drink and ordered another, pressing her to join him. The two lads walked out without saying goodnight and the policeman moved across to the table they'd vacated and picked up the evening paper. Paul settled himself comfortably on his stool.

'How are *you*?' he asked, and prepared himself to listen with simulated interest to an account of her new life in Yorkshire, with oblique references to wealth and perquisites, and more direct allusions to racing and bloodstock, dinner parties and names which were dropped with embarrassing frequency in the quietude of the bar. He remembered to register awe with each Honourable and hyphen and was rewarded with whisky as a dog is tossed sugar.

The hands of the clock above the bar moved with surprising speed. At a quarter to ten the policeman rose and said goodnight, going upstairs to a room next to Lynch's, so Olive told him.

When he'd gone they looked at each other in silence.

'I've had rather a lot to drink,' he said.

'Yes, sweetie.' She hadn't been stinting her own share. 'Perhaps you ought to leave your gorgeous motor and walk home. I'm afraid I can't offer you a bed. We have only three bedrooms.'

'That's quite all right. I can drive. No traffic in this dale at night. Not much before. "Before", that's what we say now: "before". Before the deluge. Did she come in here much?'

Olive looked bewildered.

'Who, dear?'

'Judy Scroop.'

Her face, slightly shiny and vacuous, sharpened viciously.

'Not much.'

His tone was caressing:

'Who were the boy friends, ducky?'

She seemed to withdraw slightly, weighing him up.

'It wasn't Bill,' he pressed.

She sneered.

'Of course not. He hasn't the guts to kill a rat. Hasn't got the strength either. She was a strong girl.'

She looked down at her hands which rested on the bar. He followed her glance and saw the long brown fingers stretch and clench. She smiled. It was a fascinating smile; it spread to her eyes and it was most unpleasant.

'Hello,' he said in astonishment. 'Where were you on Saturday night?'

She started to laugh. It was a loud laugh and it jarred. He felt a cold spot between his shoulder blades. It was late and the fire was going down. A curtain blew inwards with the draught.

'Last Saturday evening,' Olive said, 'we never even got home. We joined a party after Catterick who were spending the night at Scotch Corner. I had an excellent alibi. I was plastered by eleven. No, sweetie, I couldn't have killed her. You'll have to find someone else.'

He stumbled on the gravel and his hands encountered something cold and smooth. With closed eyes he explored it, all his senses in his fingers. Familiar shapes registered themselves tardily on his brain but identification was a long time coming. Then he laughed. Door handle. Car. His car. He opened his eyes and saw metal points gleam in the moonlight.

'I shall walk home,' he told himself gravely. 'The night is too beautiful to be enclosed in a box.'

It was indeed a glorious night with fleets of clouds passing across the moon. It was too short a step to Foodale by way of the Street and the thought of the long way home across the Outlands seemed like an adventure. So far the evening had been exciting; he had forgotten the sequence of events but he had an impression like the memory of a dream: it had been exciting. To walk home up the empty Street and Foodale would be dull. There would be foxes but who wanted to listen to foxes? He wanted Ruth and Ruth wanted someone else unless he could prove Ned guilty. No, that was wrong. To prove someone *else* guilty. Who? He'd forgotten. All he could remember was that it was essential to find the body. It had become an obsession.

He turned right on the main road and started to walk past Bull Low. When he came to the quarry he went up the incline, walking through the thin pale mud.

He hadn't liked it before. He smiled. It wasn't deep enough to matter: just an inch or two. Underneath was a hard surface. It was only dirt and would brush off, or he could buy new shoes and slacks. It felt rather nice, like walking through cream, and less greasy.

The incline was well lit but there was no one about and no lorries passed. Ahead and above he heard the quarry working: the night shift for the voracious motorways. He grimaced in horror: England was slowly stifling under a concrete blanket. Ned had it right: people weren't important; it was the land mattered most: corn and trees and hedgerows, all vanishing under the legions of combine harvesters and earth movers and a million tons of rock blasted in a thousand quarries every week. Figures wrong, he thought, but they could be adjusted. He remembered his projected film and a wave of euphoria washed over him. He pictured a shot at night, looking down from the top of the face. Must go up there—now. Not too close, he cautioned himself; could be dangerous. Not quite sober; watch it, lad.

The gradient eased. He was near the offices and the hoppers where the lorries were loaded. One was there now, being sheeted. Against the continuous background of noise, the little men appeared to move soundlessly, adjusting the huge tarpaulin, roping it on cleats. From under the thick cover steam rose in gasps like those of an expiring animal.

Unchallenged and almost unnoticed, he watched from the dead ground between two lamps, then turned and plodded up the track that led to the top.

He was sweating a little and he slowed down. He wasn't thinking now; the physical strain, the effort to stay on his feet, precluded thought. Everything that happened was a matter of sensation: grass and stones under his feet instead of smooth mud, air on his face as he climbed higher, a curiously heavy silence as the sound of the quarry receded because the track curved in a great hairpin and then came back, always climbing, until he emerged on the cold clear upland of the plateau.

Below, a flood of diffused light and a murmurous sound rose from the pit. He left the track and advanced towards the top of the face where he stopped, a few feet back from the edge. Underneath him the quarry groaned and clanked and hummed, flooded by the inexorable lights. He saw the Euclids, their shining metal shrouded by dust, speeding like furry crabs to the crusher. He heard the boulders crash on the rock-strewn apron.

He watched the chains stroke the rocks as they moved down the belt to the impact breaker and he stared at the little box and visualised the power inside.

Beyond the crusher a rising belt bore lumps like chalk, the size of a fist—and in the end it was an eighth of an inch in diameter. Not so drunk, he thought, chuckling, but he stopped. For a second time that night he felt cold between his shoulder blades.

'Good evening,' a voice said, also amused.

He started to turn and a hand drew him back from the edge.

'What are *you* doing here?'

'We could go down Styx now, if you want.'

'Your name's not Charon. But you're right; no time like the present. It'll complete the evening.'

*   *   *

It was different from what he'd imagined. There was no sense of claustrophobia and the lights brought by his guide seemed very powerful. There was no climbing either; he'd thought that cavers performed similar feats to those of rock climbers, but underground. He found that progress was on roughly the same level: safe, but often extremely strenuous. For much of the time they couldn't walk upright. Once they lay down and did a tortuous shuffle, feet first, along an angled slit which couldn't have been more than a foot high.

They emerged in a chamber and there was a raw cold smell which was strange to him. Far up in the ceiling he caught a glimpse of toffee-coloured pelmets. He must have been almost asleep on his feet; for a moment he thought he was at the theatre—the opera perhaps? The silence was profound.

He was urged onwards and his feet trod soft silt, then stone. He splashed in water. It deepened and he stopped, appalled. But his companion was plodding on, deeper, water thrashing the walls of a passage, the light glaring ahead of him: a tiny receding world. He hurried after, frustrated by the resistance of the water which was over his knees. It was pleasantly cool.

He was reminded of his childhood, even more so when they turned aside and the roof came down so that first they had to crawl on hands and knees, and then lie prone in a few inches of water and wriggle down a long bedding plane which slanted alarmingly. The water rushed past his face now and ahead he could hear it on rocks.

So far as topography went he was lost and completely dependent on the other. He didn't care. He had only just enough strength left to draw himself out of the low passage and stand up. His light showed him a chamber floored with glutinous mud from which monstrous stalagmites bulged. There were the shells of fossils embedded

191

in the walls and the roof was a fantastic drapery of caramel straws. Everything was in shades of brown and shone.

They came to a pool which was roughly square with sides about six feet long. It was surprisingly clear. They stood on a tiny beach and by the light of the torches they could see a wall dropping into the water and just below the surface was the lintel of a submerged passage.

This was pointed out to him and he nodded solemnly.

'Take a deep breath,' his guide said. 'Swim six strokes —count them carefully as you go—then surface. You'll be on the other side then, in the chamber.'

'And that's where he's hidden the body?'

'That's where I reckon she is. We'll see. I had to have a witness and you're from outside. Now, the important thing to remember is six: count to six.'

'Six,' he repeated. He was silent for a moment, then he asked:

'Is this a sump?'

'No, this is a "duck"; you just duck down for a moment, see. The sump's right up other end, miles away.'

'What shall I do about my glasses?'

'Leave them here.'

'I'm blind without them.'

'I'll bring them then; you won't need them till you surface. The headlamps will go on working underwater. Off you go. I'll be right behind you.'

He was soaked through already so it didn't seem all that cold; in fact, the deep water was preferable to the slimy stuff in the passages, and clammy clothes on his skin.

The pool shelved steeply. If he could swim through the passage it must be capacious, about seven feet in diameter, perhaps. Did he do a breast stroke or a dog paddle? What did it matter? It was only a few feet. If he took a deep breath and plunged in head first, impetus should carry him through.

The light was shining on the top of the water now so he couldn't see the lintel but he knew where it was: about twelve inches below the surface. He stood still, took a deep breath, and dived.

It wasn't so clear after all; he must have stirred up silt—but he was in the passage, otherwise he'd have struck the wall of the pool. He was so short-sighted that all he could see was light, and movement in the brown water.

He'd forgotten to count so he started at three, swimming breast stroke because the passage was quite wide. Four. He hadn't touched a wall yet. Five. Ah, there was something; he felt it with his foot. Six. He was exhaling slowly. Now up.

His head struck rock. God, he wasn't through! He hadn't gone far enough. He felt his way along the roof quickly. Quicker to swim? No, direction was better by feel; he liked the rock under his hands.

How would he know when he was through? Would his hands be able to feel the air? Where was the air? He hadn't got much time left. Murder, he thought; I deserve it.

His light went out.

Chapter 14

'WHERE DO YOU think he's gone?' Laura asked, staring curiously at the empty space where the Bentley had stood.

'He could be anywhere.'

Ruth moved across the terrace to look down Foodale. No car lights were visible.

'What's he after?'

'He's trying to prove Ned's innocence.'

'Why? He's not all that friendly towards Ned.'

'No. He's doing it for me.'

'God!' Laura exclaimed. 'It's all sex, isn't it?'

'Get away,' Ruth said absently. 'Nearly everything is when you come down to it.'

'Is that so? I'll get back to John. If Paul's there, I'll send him home.'

'He can't be. He's gone some distance if he's taken the car. Good night, and thanks for coming over. I feel better now.'

She left the side door open, the outer light on, and went to bed. It was midnight.

She slept surprisingly well and woke at half past seven. There was a strong tang of coffee and she went downstairs in her dressing gown to find her daughter alone in the kitchen.

'Good morning.' Susan looked at her mother with

194

sympathy. 'Coffee? What happened to Paul?'

'Isn't he back?'

'He may be. His car isn't.'

'He went off some time last evening—' On an impulse she ran upstairs, but the guest room was empty and the bed hadn't been slept in. His suit case was on the bed, open but with only the sponge bag removed and lying on the quilt, as he must have left it yesterday afternoon when he arrived. She returned to the kitchen.

'Laura went very late,' she said, 'and the Bentley wasn't there then. He must have crept out, on the scent.'

'What scent?'

'He doesn't think Ned's guilty.'

'Well, of course he isn't.'

'Do you know who is?'

'No idea.'

Susan ate with a good appetite and left to catch the school bus. Ruth bathed and dressed, and Annie Hibbert arrived. Ruth wondered what to do about lunch and wished Paul had left a note saying where he was going and when he would be back. Failing that, why didn't he telephone?

She wandered aimlessly about the house and by ten o'clock she was confused, her thoughts starting to gyrate in circles drawn between fixed points: Ned, Paul, murder, suspicion, Judy, disappearances. So many people were disappearing. Olive had come back and the explanation for her absence was innocuous. On the other hand, there was blood on a barn door, and too much in the cobbles for Judy to be alive. And Paul? Had he become involved in violence too? She panicked. He'd vanished like the others. She forgot there could be an innocent explanation (accident, amnesia); she had the feeling that they were being picked off one by one. A

195

malignant force was at work; there was no escape.

She was in the sitting room. She collapsed on the sofa and leaned back, breathing deeply. Deliberately she refrained from drinking. She must concentrate, and work from basic principles, from scratch. It was less important at this moment to establish the reason for his absence than to recover her own equilibrium. Activity was the way to do this. So she would try to trace him, merely as an exercise.

She began to think of it as a problem in detection. Where was the start? That was obvious. It lay with the person who had seen him last. She put on a coat and went through the wood to Yaffles.

Laura said that John was at the surgery. She didn't know what Paul and he had talked about last night; he'd been asleep when she got home and this morning they hadn't discussed it in front of the boys. Then Marilyn had arrived so she hadn't seen John alone since yesterday.

Ruth walked down Foodale where a robin sang on a fence post and some old red oaks grew redder every day. Pretty, she thought, hurrying down the lane; he came this way last night—or did he? She stopped, swung round and stared across the ravine towards Jagger's. Should she go there? But no; he'd taken the Bentley—so he hadn't gone to the barn.

She continued quickly to Bardale, past Styx Hole where frost was thawing and trees dripped dolefully on Hibbert's garage, past his cottage where curtains were drawn behind an open bedroom window, then Michael's cottage: closed curtains and closed windows. Mrs Padley waved from behind the old-fashioned sweet jars and, next door to the surgery, Henry sat at the open window, muffled to the chin and wheezing gaily.

She hesitated, then remembered that he would have

been in bed at the relevant times. She didn't stop but called a greeting, then turned in at the door of the surgery.

It was twenty past ten and there was no one in the waiting room. No one was with John either, for as she closed the street door loudly, letting him know that he had a visitor, she heard steps in the inner room, and the door opened.

They faced each other across the shabby carpet.

'Something wrong?' he asked.

'Paul didn't come home last night.'

He didn't move to invite her inside; this was no leisurely consultation.

'I have to find him,' she said, and now she acknowledged the urgency; it wasn't an academic exercise, it never had been. 'He was determined to find out the truth. He had an incentive. Probably he discovered something very quickly that gave him a lead.' Her tone sharpened. 'Nothing happens in this place without everyone knowing in five minutes. He found out something, John; they've got him.'

'Oh, there's no *gang*!' He appeared shocked. He threw her a sharp glance, crossed the room and bolted the outer door. 'Right, we'll discuss it.'

'We haven't time.'

'Not exhaustively. Tell me why you think he's missing.'

She told him about the Bentley being gone and that his bed hadn't been slept in.

'He went while Laura was with me—after he'd visited you,' she told him.

John said slowly:

'He was gunning for the Hibberts, for Michael in particular, when he left me. I tried to put him off.'

'You think he went straight to Michael?'

'That's easy enough to find out. I'll ask Marilyn; she's at Yaffles.'

No, Marilyn said, Mr Trevena hadn't come to see them last night; she hadn't known that he was back in Bardale.

'Could he have hung about till Michael went to work?' Ruth asked as John replaced the receiver.

'He left me about eight so he'd have two hours to wait before Michael left home. He'd never wait in the Street. He could have gone to the Woman.'

'Don't trouble to ring,' Ruth said. 'I'll go and see.'

'I'll try Emily,' she heard him say as she struggled with the bolt on the street door.

'Yes,' Olive said coldly, mutely disapproving because Ruth hadn't asked after Bill. 'Paul called here—and spent some time, in fact.' She touched her hair self-consciously. 'We had quite a party.'

'What time did he leave?'

'At closing time; I didn't notice exactly.'

'Why didn't he take his car?'

'He was somewhat under the weather. The Bentley was quite safe here.' Her resentment at Ruth's tone was defeated by human curiosity and the other woman's intensity.

'What's happened?' she asked.

Ruth looked at her bleakly.

'He hasn't come home.'

'But he could walk! He wasn't incapable by any means.'

She appeared outraged to think that the possibility of a drunk reeling out of the Woman could become a matter for gossip in Bardale. She hesitated.

'The river?' she asked tentatively.

'How much did he have to drink?'

There were steps outside and John Eden came in.

'He wasn't sober when he arrived,' Olive said, nodding to the doctor and including him in the conversation: 'I'd say he'd had a good bit to drink somewhere.'

'He had,' John told them. 'He'd been at Emily's, and she'd given him some of her home-made stuff. That's potent. He'd be drunk when he left here. Emily's coming down,' he added, turning to Ruth.

'Did he leave alone?' he asked Olive.

'Yes. There was no one else in the bar.'

Despite herself, Ruth was reminded of the circumstances of Judy's disappearance and how, at first, they'd remarked that there was only the proprietor's word for it that the girl had actually left the bar. She stared at Olive intently.

'There were two lads in earlier, probably from Bull Low,' the woman said quickly, sensing the atmosphere, 'and a policeman. He slept on the premises.'

'What did you talk about?' John asked.

'I beg your pardon?'

'With Mr Trevena. You must have talked. He could talk, couldn't he?'

'We exchanged gossip.'

'No,' Ruth said tightly. 'He was looking for the murderer. He would be asking leading questions. Try to remember some of them.'

The woman's face held a flat vicious look which Ruth had noticed before but never identified until that moment. Olive glanced down at her hands and smiled.

'He wanted to know who Judy Scroop's friends were.'

'What did you say?'

'How would I know? Her life didn't concern me. My husband couldn't have killed her. It's a police matter.'

There was a sound of light tyres on gravel and Emily

Jebb could be seen propping her bicycle against the wall.

'Where is he?' she asked, as she came in the bar.

John explained as much as they knew. Ruth wondered at the speed with which he'd grasped the situation. Emily listened, not interrupting, her hands thrust deep in the pockets of her old camouflaged jacket. When he'd finished, she turned to Olive Lynch.

'For how long before ten o'clock had you and Mr Trevena been alone in the bar?'

'Over half an hour.'

'And no one called, just slipped in for cigarettes, say?'

Olive was definite that she had seen no one other than Paul after the policeman went to bed—and the Bull Low boys had left about half an hour before him. She'd been tired, wanting to go upstairs herself. Really, she'd been waiting for Paul to leave. She'd let the fire go down and opened the window, hoping the chill would drive him home.

'When did you open the window?' Emily asked.

Olive drew herself up but no one facing her was intimidated.

'When the policeman went up: about a quarter to ten.'

'And you were talking about the murder,' Emily said reproachfully.

'Well, it was a topic of conversation, wasn't it?'

Emily took a sudden decision and turned to John.

'Get that man Quinney here with a team and diving equipment,' she said. 'Quickly. Tell him why.'

John nodded and left the room. Olive followed him.

'No,' Ruth breathed, staring at Emily.

'I'm sorry,' the old woman murmured.

'How—what makes you think he's in the sump?'

'Because he was so interested in Styx. I told him the police would have searched the sump yesterday, that the body couldn't be in it, but I told him where it led: to the New Series. He might have tried to get through. How well does he swim?'

'Very well. Extremely well. He's done a lot of diving on holidays.'

Emily said nothing. They were both thinking of the length of the sump.

'Not well enough,' Ruth added hopelessly.

Emily raised her eyebrows in tacit agreement.

'But he'd never go there alone, even if he was drunk!' the younger woman protested suddenly.

'He may not have gone alone. That's what we're worried about. I know how his mind works,' Emily said quietly.

'Whose mind? Who took him? The murderer?'

'Which murderer?' Emily asked, and there was a world of fatigue in her voice.

'There's more than one? What are you talking about?' Ruth's voice mounted dangerously.

'Pull yourself together,' Emily said, quick but not unkindly. 'Not that it matters what Olive Lynch knows now. But you mustn't lose your grip.'

Olive came back then and said that Quinney was coming straight away.

'Where's John?' Ruth asked, with the grasshopper curiosity that accompanies shock.

'Gone out,' the woman told her, pouring brandy. She placed three glasses on the bar. 'Drink up,' she said. 'You look as though you need it.'

The tone roused Ruth. She sipped the drink carefully, feeling the wheels slowly start to turn again: the wheels of reason. The three women were silent, waiting and thinking.

'Can't we do anything?' Ruth asked as the clock ticked away the minutes.

'No. We have to wait for the experts.'

'Suppose he's just broken his leg or something?'

'In that case it won't hurt him to wait a little longer.'

Through the window they saw Hibbert's Land Rover turn in to the pub. Ruth heard Emily sigh beside her. John Eden got out of the passenger seat. Olive lit a cigarette and her hand shook. John entered the bar looking grim.

'We're going in by the quarry entrance,' he said. 'We can go as far as the sump anyway. Tell Quinney to come straight in at this end.'

Emily nodded.

'I'll do that. Where is the other one?'

'Gone. We broke in.'

He turned and went out. As they drove away Ruth said dully:

'He means Michael Hibbert, doesn't he? It was Michael listening outside this window, on his way to work. John said Paul was gunning for him.'

'Yes,' Emily agreed. 'It would be Michael who heard you discussing the murder.' She was looking at Olive.

The woman flushed.

'We didn't discuss anything. He had the impertinence to ask me where *I* was last Saturday night.'

'Where were you?' Ruth asked without much interest.

'At Scotch Corner.'

'Look,' Ruth said to Emily. 'John isn't experienced. If he can go down Styx, why can't we?'

'We'll be in the way, my dear. John is a doctor, and Joe can't look after more than one person.'

'How can they go in anyway, without ropes?' Ruth sounded petulant.

'It's the other entrance by Joe's garage where you

have to do the climbing,' Emily explained. 'At this end the entrance is on roughly the same level as the sump and the passages are horizontal. You don't need ropes.'

There was a long silence broken by Ruth again:

'You implied there were two murderers,' she said, harking back.

Emily wouldn't meet her eyes. Olive's mouth hung open slightly.

'Two,' Ruth repeated. 'If Michael's killed Paul, that's one. You mean someone else killed Judy.' Her glance came round to Olive Lynch.

'No,' the woman said quickly. 'I was at Scotch Corner. I can prove it.'

'It wasn't Mrs Lynch,' Emily murmured automatically, staring at the sunshine on top of the cliffs across the road. 'Come along,' she said suddenly. 'We'll go to the quarry entrance.'

'You're evading the question,' Ruth accused as they walked past Bull Low.

Emily answered without pausing in her stride but this time she met Ruth's eye.

'I can't talk now,' she said. 'And it doesn't matter who killed Judy. I tried to impress that on Paul and so did John. We failed—and this is the result. D'you see: we were trying to *protect* Paul. We knew the danger he was in. He was too clever and he knew us too well—unlike the police.'

'He found out.' Ruth stopped and looked back towards the Quiet Woman. Emily took her arm and urged her towards the quarry.

'Think of Paul,' she said tensely. 'There may still be a chance for him. Judy doesn't matter now.'

'There's Ned too,' Ruth mused as she allowed herself to be chivvied along by the older woman, but neither of them followed this thread. There no longer appeared to be any urgency about Ned's position.

They turned off the main road at the quarry entrance and a vehicle slowed behind them. It was a black Cortina. Quinney was driving. Neill, in the passenger seat, lifted a hand but the car didn't stop until it had gone a few yards up the quarry incline when it lurched over the kerb and halted on the grass verge behind Hibbert's Land Rover. A number of men got out and among them was Ned Stanton who walked back towards them.

He looked at them quizzically.

'Any news?' he asked.

'It depends on what you know,' Emily said. 'Have they released you?'

He nodded morosely.

'No evidence.'

'I wish I'd known yesterday that you didn't do it,' Ruth said.

'You thought I killed Judy?' He looked surprised.

'You did your best to make me think so. That's why Paul's been— that's why he's missing.'

Ned looked uncomfortable.

'I didn't know this would happen.'

'We did warn Paul,' Emily pointed out.

'Did you tell him,' Ruth asked, 'that if he persisted in trying to discover the truth, he would be stopped; that a person who'd killed once wouldn't hesitate to kill a second time to protect himself?'

'But—' Ned began, to be interrupted by Emily:

'No, no one told him that—'

'Mr Stanton!' Neill's voice came from the group farther up the track. Ned returned to the police.

'Where's the entrance?' Ruth asked.

'In a cave at the foot of that wall.'

Emily pointed to a crag visible through the trees near

the Cortina. A Dormobile came up the road and stopped behind the police vehicle. Men tumbled out of it, wearing boiler suits and carrying helmets. Some were in wet suits. Gear and metal cylinders were handed out and a curious contraption like a long wicker basket was laid on the grass.

'My God!' Ruth exclaimed, thinking it was a kind of coffin.

'It's only a stretcher,' Emily said.

Ruth turned and looked over the dale.

'Do you know where he's gone?' she asked.

'Who, dear?'

'Michael Hibbert.'

'To London, I expect. It's the place a petty criminal would make for, to lose himself.'

'You think of Michael as a *petty* criminal?' Ruth asked conversationally.

The steel-rimmed spectacles turned on her blandly: 'Yes. Basically he's nothing more.'

Technically, he wasn't. He hadn't killed Paul Trevena, and Paul's swimming ability had been just good enough. Quinney found him, still alive, seventy feet inside the sump, crouched in a curious little niche in the one place where the roof lifted for a foot or two, enough to accommodate a small man. They brought him out with the breathing apparatus.

Ruth and the others watched him being transferred to the waiting ambulance. Everyone was quiet and numb with relief, and Paul appeared to have lapsed into unconsciousness.

'He'll live,' John called cheerfully as the ambulance doors were shut on him. The others turned away and walked slowly down the track. Ruth paused once, longing to sit down on the grass, but Ned and Emily insisted on her continuing. She was aware of a peculiar urgency in the air. Neill and Quinney had disappeared.

Chapter 15

'HA!' HENRY RAVEN exclaimed. 'Back again then?'
The Stantons stopped and regarded him.

'I'm back,' Ned said superfluously. 'And young Hibbert's gone. Did *you* know that there was a place halfway along the Styx sump where a man could crawl out and wait to be rescued?'

Henry's eyes glittered with interest.

'That I didn't. Who crawled out?'

'Mr Trevena.'

'Ha. He be a lucky man then. He'd never have the same luck again. People don't realise dangers unless they be born here.'

'That's right. He knows now.'

'He don't want to make no fillum here neither,' Henry said.

'He won't,' Ned assured him.

They walked on. They had to walk because the Bentley was locked and there was no other car from Foodale in the Street. Emily had ridden ahead on her bicycle and with her departure the sense of urgency had gone.

There was a broken pane in the window of the young Hibberts' parlour.

'I'll send for the glazier to mend that,' Ned said. 'It looks bad.'

'So does Michael's disappearance.'

'I was thinking of Marilyn coming home and finding her cottage broken into.'

There was no one visible next door and Joe's garage was open and empty.

'Where can Annie be?' Ned asked.

'She's at Heathens'.'

'No! How long has she been there?'

'Why, since nine o'clock. She's been coming all this week. Had you forgotten?'

Ned said nothing but quickened his pace up Foodale.

'I can't keep up,' Ruth gasped. 'Slow down a bit.'

He glanced at her, looked up the hill, hesitating, then he gave her his arm and they strolled up the lane at a moderate speed. The robin was still singing on the fence post, or he'd been away and come back. There was an old gate on the right, below the Yaffles entrance. He drew her aside and leaned on the top bar. They could hear the brook talking to itself among the rocks below.

'Suppose,' he began, sounding casual, 'that Sue were a little older and she was infatuated with a very nasty type, someone who was making her terribly unhappy, who you were convinced was driving her into a breakdown. What would you do?'

She stared at him wide eyed.

'What *is* this? Sue! It's not possible!'

'Darling! It's academic—a hypothesis.'

She looked at him doubtfully.

'Not totally irrelevant?'

'No.'

'But Sue is in no kind of trouble?'

'Not to my knowledge. But imagine it. You have the ability to put yourself in other people's places. Imagine your child suffering at the hands of someone you were convinced was evil.'

'A man using Sue—criminally? I'd kill him.'

Ned smiled at her and nodded to himself. He took her hand and drew it through his arm.

'Come on,' he said. 'We'll go home.'

Emily was waiting in the sitting room. Annie stood by the window with her back to the light.

'Did you see the police?' Emily asked.

'No,' Ned told her. 'I don't know where they are.'

'Joe will be keeping them,' Annie said.

Emily and Ned exchanged glances.

Ruth asked of Annie:

'Was it Joe killed Judy?'

No one answered her.

'Are you going to tell me?' she asked, looking from one to the other.

'We have to tell you,' Emily admitted. 'You have all the salient facts and when you've recovered from the shocks of the last few days, you'll realise the truth. We have to stop you blurting it out to the police before you've managed to get a grip on yourself again.'

'I know the truth?'

'As soon as you can put two and two together.'

'It *was* Joe then?'

'No,' Annie said. 'It was me.'

Only Ruth looked at her. The others averted their gaze and studied the fire, waiting. However, after a moment's silence Emily sighed and said gently:

'Sit down, Annie.'

'I'm happy standing, mum.'

'Would you rather I told Mrs Stanton?' Emily asked.

'I don't mind.' Annie turned to Ruth. 'What do you want to know?'

Ruth said weakly:

209

'I don't know where to start. You're all crowding me.'

'Yes,' Annie said sympathetically. 'You've had a lot of shocks one way and another.'

'Motive is the first thing,' Ned reminded his wife.

Ruth asked obediently:

'Why did you do it, Annie?'

'She were pestering my Michael.'

'But—'

'There was a lot of infatuation there,' Ned interrupted.

Ruth threw him a glance.

'Are you sure you want to go on with this, Annie?' she asked.

'You don't like asking questions, mum. No need to. Marilyn told me how things were, see, so I asked our Michael and he owned up. Said he couldn't get away from her. Met her o' nights up in the old barn. He told Marilyn he went drinking with his mates but she found out, o' course. They can never hide it.

'I went in to see him last Saturday morning when Marilyn was up here, and I told him I'd deal with it. I thought I'd be waiting for her when she come up to the barn. I was going to put the fear of death in her so she'd never trouble my boy again. I sent him to Sheffield out of the way. I wanted her to myself.

'I waited all day, thinking about her. I was alone that afternoon and evening with himself on the two to ten shift. Before ten I come up the lane here to the Outlands and I went in the barn and left the door open. She come quite prompt. She stood in the doorway and called to him. That's when I hit her.'

She stopped as if there was nothing more to say.

'How many times did you hit her?' Ruth asked.

'Just the once.'

'What with?'

'The chopper.'

'You took it with you.'

Ruth was beginning to feel herself on some kind of familiar ground and Emily looked at her sharply.

'I must have done,' Annie said with composure. 'I didn't know I had it though till she showed in the doorway. I got the scent of her. Then I felt it; the shaft fitted nice in my hand.'

Ruth nodded.

'What did you do with her then?'

'Nothing. I left her and went home and told Joe. He did the rest.'

'That explains it.' Ruth leaned back on the sofa, very tired. 'There were two people concerned. It never occurred to us—to me, nor I suppose, to the police—that a woman could have done it, because of the difficulty of disposing of the body.... Where is it, by the way?'

'I don't know.' She looked uneasy for the first time. 'Can I make a cup of tea now?'

Ruth looked inquiringly at Emily.

'Yes, you do that,' the older woman said. 'You've managed very well, Annie.'

'Thank you, mum.'

'What's going to happen to her?' Ruth asked when the woman had gone.

'Well, no one knows except us,' Ned pointed out.

'But you can't keep it from the police indefinitely.'

'We've not done badly so far. They've no inkling —and now, of course, they'll be chasing Michael. He's done us a good turn.'

'By trying to kill Paul?' Ruth's tone was dangerous.

'No, by running away. He's a fool.'

'He's a monster!'

'Don't argue about Michael now.' Emily recalled them sharply. 'He's serving a useful purpose at the moment, as Ned says, by drawing attention away from Bardale.'

'Has it occurred to you,' Ruth asked, 'that he left because he thought Paul was dead, not in order to divert attention from his mother?'

'It's immaterial why he left,' Emily insisted. 'We're all very glad Paul survived, but for whatever reason Michael ran away, his going has great advantages for his mother and the rest of us.'

'Why the rest of us?'

Emily raised her eyebrows.

'We are all accomplices in some sense.'

'You all knew?'

'Some of us—and those who didn't know guessed at least part of the truth. Some of us helped materially; I understand that that is tantamount to being an accomplice after the fact. Joe brought her clothes to me and I burned them in my furnace on Sunday morning. He put the stuff that wouldn't burn easily, zips and buttons and so on, in one of the quarry kilns. I also sent for Ned on Sunday afternoon, ostensibly to clear my gutters of dead leaves but in fact, to tell him what had happened. We talked about the story we should tell if the police came. We thought they wouldn't, but unfortunately we reckoned without the coincidence of Olive Lynch being missing at the same time, or appearing to be missing. I don't think the police would have been at all troubled if only Judy had disappeared. They would have assumed she'd gone away with a man, and doubtless we could have thought up some account of a mythical boy friend from Sheffield or even farther afield. But two women disappearing with an apparent common denominator—Bill Lynch—was too much for the police to stomach and then Renishaw's find of the lipstick brought you in, my dear. The trouble with the whole affair has been that we are all so inter-related in Bardale. Everything we do has repercussions on the others. Of course, in some cases we were able to turn this to good advantage: in our little conspiracy to convince the police of Ned's "guilt" for example. And if we hadn't been successful there, it appears that John Eden, without a word from us, was ready to step into the breach and play his part: as a suspect without an alibi and one who had a lot to lose if he were being blackmailed.'

'You weren't having an affair with her?' Ruth turned to Ned in bewilderment.

He shrugged and grimaced. He was embarrassed.

She frowned helplessly, shook her head as if to clear it, and went off on another tack.

'Judy wasn't pestering Michael, was she?'

'Dear me, no.' Emily was quite definite. 'Michael is a silly boy. His mother knows the truth but she's twisted it in her mind. She really believes Judy was infatuated with her son but you see, if that had been the truth, Annie wouldn't have killed her.'

Ruth was astonished at the old woman's perspicacity. Emily returned her stare without wavering.

'I tried to reason with Judy,' she went on. 'You see, it wasn't one man but many, and often in the same place. I knew all about the barn and I sent for her on the Saturday to have a serious talk with her. Eventually I felt she must go beyond the limits of—tolerance. Someone would object, and violently. Unfortunately Judy had no judgement, and, as she said to me, she didn't run after men, they just came.'

Ned shifted in his chair but they didn't look at him.

'If you're determined to go ahead with this,' Ruth told them, 'I hope someone has remembered to dispose of the chopper.'

'Only the handle,' Ned told her. 'Joe burned it out in

the fire, fixed a new one and put the chopper in the river for a few days.'

'Joe was busy,' Ruth commented coldly. 'He let the bullocks in the yard, of course.'

'Yes, that was Joe.'

Annie came in on the last word but she made no remark. She put down the tea tray and stood back.

'There's enough of the cold lamb for three, mum,' she said. 'And shall I open a tin of pears?'

Ruth nodded wordlessly and Annie went back to the kitchen.

She started to pour out the tea and stopped.

'What on earth are we doing drinking tea at lunch time?' she asked.

'Annie's universal panacea,' Emily reminded her.

'What are you going to do?' Ned asked of his wife.

'I? What can I do? You mean, am I going to the police? I don't think so.'

She did think about it while they waited politely.

'No, I shan't go to the police,' she resumed. She looked at them in wonder. 'Why should I? It's not my business.'

Emily smiled.

'Well done,' she said. 'They'd only put Annie in an institution and she would become withdrawn and eventually go mad. She won't kill again, of course. She'll come to accept Michael's absence and make a hero of him in her mind. She'll stay in Bardale and live out her life contentedly with her work, and the grandchild and Joe. She's quite harmless.'

'No revenge,' Ruth said.

'No dear. No one will avenge Judy. Poor girl, she brought it on herself.'

'We all did that,' Ned put in. 'Everyone acted in character.'

'But everyone always does,' Emily said in surprise.

'Not Paul,' Ruth reminded them. 'He must have had the death wish to go in that sump.'

'Now that's a thought!' Ned turned to her in surprise. 'But he had more healthy reasons as well. He was able to tell Quinney before he was brought out. He couldn't remember much because he'd been very drunk. At least, that's what Quinney said, but I wonder if Paul knows a lot more than he appears to, and is covering up. He was insistent that it was Michael with him in the cave and that the lad tried to kill him, the implication being that Paul was on to the truth and Michael tried to silence him to protect himself.'

'Why shouldn't that be what Paul really thinks—as if it matters?' Ruth asked.

'Oh, it matters,' Ned rejoined. 'For one thing, if Paul had thought Michael was the killer, he'd never have gone in the cave with him, but also—and more serious for Annie—if Paul's on to the truth, he'll have to be silenced.'

'He knew Michael was innocent,' Emily said. 'I told him.'

'That's why he trusted Michael then,' Ned pointed out. 'What he didn't realise was that even if Michael wasn't the original murderer, he was dangerous because he could kill to protect his mother.'

'He didn't know it was Annie,' Ruth told them. 'He was thinking in terms of Olive when he left the pub.'

'*Olive!* Why?' Ned was amused.

'He asked her where she'd been last Saturday night.'

'Would Michael know that? It was only a step to considering another woman as the murderer.'

'It was around ten o'clock,' Emily told him. 'The window was open and Michael would be on his way to work. He's as inquisitive as a monkey and Paul's car was outside the pub.'

'He was drunk too,' Ned mused. 'Thinking about Olive would side-track him from the Hibberts, except to think that Michael could show him where the body was. Paul insisted to Quinney that the body is in the New Series. If they believe him they'll concentrate down there, although one can't imagine how a body could be got through that sump without breathing apparatus, and Michael's no diver. Perhaps they'll look for another way in to the New Series.'

Emily and Ned smiled at each other.

'Is she there?' Ruth asked.

'No.' It was Ned who answered her. 'But Paul thought so last night. That's why he went in the water. Being drunk and a novice, he got all confused, and Michael must have led him a hell of a dance to get there. The sump's not far from that entrance but he says that they seemed to travel an enormous distance.

'When they came to the pool, Michael said it led to the New Series all right, but that it was a "duck" of only a few feet—that the sump was at the other end of the system. He said Paul should submerge and swim, count up to six, then surface.'

'That was wicked,' Emily said.

Ruth looked at her with interest. The old woman returned the look.

'No,' she said as if in answer. 'I do not condone that. Annie had some justification but Michael went too far. He will not come back to Bardale.'

'He would if his mother were charged,' Ruth said.

'She won't be.' Emily's tone held conviction.

'There is the body,' Ruth pointed out. 'They're so expert they'll not only identify the weapon that made the injury as a chopper, they'll actually fit the Hibberts' chopper to the wound.'

'They can't do that,' Emily said.

''Look.' Ruth was exasperated. 'What have you done with her? Lime? That preserves bodies. And if she's even in an unexplored part of Styx Hole, a caver will find her eventually. If she's blocked up in a passage, don't you realise that everyone will be on the lookout for that kind of thing? You don't stand a chance.'

'The body doesn't exist,' Emily said.

'Well, not exactly correct,' Ned demurred. 'But there's no question of tracing how she died nor who killed her.'

'Lime preserves tissues,' Ruth repeated in stubborn fatigue.

'The impact breaker doesn't.'

'The impact—! The *crusher*?'

He nodded.

'Joe and Michael were on the ten to six shift on Sunday. Joe left the body just inside the woods by the barn on Saturday night and went up early with the Land Rover on Sunday morning. No one would take any notice; he was out all hours of the day and night, on foot and in the 'Rover, watching birds or badgers or something. She was there in his garage all day Sunday till he went to work in the evening. He went on using the 'Rover to go to work in after the police arrived because he needed it under his eyes. He didn't want them poking about in the back, taking dirt away to be analysed.'

She stared at him in dawning comprehension.

'They'd have to take up the motorway!'

'My dear girl, what would it matter? The fragments are one-eighth of an inch! Even if they suspected, are they really going to spend thousands, perhaps millions of pounds, digging it up, cleaning it, analysing it, when they know they can never prove what happened to Judy Scroop?'

'The *silly* girl!' Ruth burst out. 'Her instincts didn't help her when it came to other women, did they?'

They had forgotten Emily. Now she rose.

'If you'll excuse me,' she said to Ruth, 'I'll get back to the animals. I'm glad we've talked.' It was as if they'd been discussing some minor problem that concerned their mutual boundary. 'I suggest you have a couple of stiff brandies and then a good nap.'

'How much does Sue know of all this?' Ruth asked when Emily had gone and they were following her advice regarding the brandy.

'She'll be all right.'

'What do you mean: "she'll be all right"? What does she know?'

'Virtually everything, I expect.'

'She said that yesterday. I thought she was exaggerating. You don't mean she knows Annie is—a murderer?'

'Sure to. She couldn't not know. It won't hurt her. Some of them have got stamina.'

'Some of who?'

'Bardale. There's a degenerate streak in Michael, but look at the spirit in Henry and Emily and Joe.'

'It's frightening,' she said. 'You're all so certain you're right. There's Emily taking the decision to let Annie stay, protected from the police, but also deciding that Michael shall be banished for ever. That's what it amounts to.'

'Do you think Annie should be surrendered to the police?'

'No.'

'Do you think Michael was justified in trying to drown Paul?'

'You know damn well I don't. He's got the mind of a killer.'

'You're all theory. You won't act on it. You're frightened of power. Emily follows through.'

'You're like her,' she said absently.

'We're related. All Bardale's related by blood or marriage.'

'What will happen to Marilyn?' she asked.

'She's far better off without him. She'll know it too. She'll marry again if only for the sake of the kid.'

'You're all so damned philosophical,' she said. 'You've got an answer for everything. Did you care for Judy?'

'No.' He returned her gaze candidly. 'She was a convenience, nothing more. Last summer meant that I met her more often, that's all.'

'Yes.' She sighed. 'Three months is a long time. Curious, that two writers can't communicate with each other. You were so deeply involved when I phoned from Yugoslavia.'

'Don't play the rejected wife; that's unworthy of you. What I told you was the truth: I had too much work. I'm afraid I'm finding the environment far more absorbing than my book, and quite frankly, I was so strung up when you rang that I resented the intrusion.'

'Go on,' she prompted.

'We used that incident—of the phone call—and my non-relationship with Judy, on which to build a plot.'

'We?'

'Emily and I. We were inter-acting all the time, doling out bits of atmosphere and fact to the police designed to make them think I was the deceiving husband afraid that his luxurious mode of life was in the balance. As I intimated to you, Judy was supposed to be my symbol of rebellion against feminine autocracy, and killing her thus became logical. I was making sure my position as a kept man stayed secure.'

219

'Good God!'

'It worked.'

'I'll say it worked. Have you ever watched people digging up a garden when you thought there was a body buried there?'

'You should have used your brain. How could I have buried a body under your open window?'

'I don't work with my brain. You know that.'

'Just as well.' He grinned. 'If you had used reason, you'd have seen it couldn't have been me, and your behaviour couldn't have supported our little conspiracy. You knew me too well.'

'Just what do you mean by that?'

'Where was my motive?'

'Perhaps,' she said carefully, 'you thought I wanted to marry Paul and that your affair with Judy gave me the opportunity for divorce.'

'Don't be silly,' he said. 'You're not going off with Paul.'

She looked at him broodingly. At length she said:

'You're quite right, I'm not. But there is the question of how we ensure his silence.'

'You can do that,' he told her. 'You're two of a kind; he'll understand when you tell him the truth. Besides, he likes Annie. It isn't such a terrible secret to keep, particularly since it doesn't really concern him. You must see that he gives up all thought of his film too. It would draw attention to the impact breaker.'

'I've under-rated you,' she observed, 'though there were some incidents. . . . You did pinch that lipstick.'

'You didn't need it. Judy liked the colour.'

'*Just* like magpies,' she said. 'Now tell me: what were you doing on Saturday night when you weren't in the study?'

'More or less as you thought. Sitting on the seat in the wood, listening to the foxes but not thinking about any book; I was working out a feature on death control.'